ALSO BY ANN MARIE SKORDY


Start with Your Heart


Soul Traveler Cards of Empowerment

In collaboration with Dana Sardano

# HAPPY HOUR

# AT

# THE WATER'S EDGE

What appears to be is not what is...

Written by

## ANN MARIE SKORDY

Phenom
PUBLISHING

First published in the U.S.A. in 2022 by

**Phenom**
PUBLISHING

A DIVISION OF THE UNIQUELY U. GROUP LLC
NEW YORK, NEW YORK

Cover and Interior Artwork by Ann Marie Skordy, Copyright © 2022
Cover and Interior Design by Angela DiMarco

First Edition 2022

ISBN 979-8-9872105-0-5

This book is dedicated to

The Butterfly of Balance et al.

# INTRODUCTION

Razzle exhaled deeply and knocked on the door.

"Come in," echoed a voice from the other side.

She gripped the heavy iron horseshoe handle, keenly aware of its cold smooth surface in her palm, and pushed the wooden archway shaped door open. She stepped across the threshold into a tiny dimly lit room, gently shutting the door behind her.

"I am Sonia," said the psychic.

"I'm Razzle Dazzle," responded the girl, eye glued to the mysterious figure of the woman sitting at the table in the corner. She was about to experience the first psychic reading of her young life, and her heart felt like it was about to explode out of her chest any second. Her best friend Sydney—who was way more savvy in these metaphysical matters than Razzle—had assured her that this woman was the real deal, and she was here to find out for herself.

"Please sit," commanded Sonia, waving her in.

Razzle practically sprinted across the room, sliding into the empty chair opposite Sonia, buzzing with excitement, utterly fascinated by the intuitive peering at her with the most unusual eyes she'd ever seen. The woman's deep-set golden irises glowed in the flickering candle light like an owl, and although she'd barely said a word yet, Razzle was certain Sonia *knew* things...things her limited brain had absolutely no comprehension of.

Sonia sat quietly appraising her client with an impassive face of indeterminable age. Likewise, her manner was equally hard to define. She appeared to be neither friendly or unfriendly, nor could she be classifies as outgoing or overly reserved either. And although she wasn't rude or curt by any stretch, on the other hand, she also wasn't what one would refer to as warm and fuzzy. In fact, it became quite clear to Razzle that this woman was poised in the center of any description she could come up with.

Sonia remained gazing at her visitor in a neutral way while expertly shuffling a deck of cards. "You are a writer."

Razzle laughed out loud. "I'm not an *anything!*" she giggled.

Sonia didn't respond. Instead she placed the deck of cards face-down in front of Razzle. "Cut these into three piles."

Suddenly consumed by nervous energy, Razzle did what she was told, watching silently as Sonia scooped up the piles and shuffled them together once more. When she stopped shuffling, she began turning the strange picture cards over, one by one, placing them on the table in a sequence and pattern that made no sense to a novice of the spiritual world. Razzle sat fixated, observing every move the woman made, mesmerized by her methods.

Completely absorbed in her task, Sonia no longer seemed conscious of her visitor's presence and continued laying out the cards. Then, as she deliberately turned the final one over, the psychic stared wide-eyed at the card spread on the table, her jaw dropping open involuntarily in an expression of undisguised astonishment.

Quickly composing herself, Sonia took a deep breath and leaned back in her chair, casually running her hands through her short blond hair, attempting to act as if the moment hadn't happened. The unrestrained display of emotion was fleeting, but from the corner of her eye she could see the girl's expression and knew she'd revealed too much. The damage was done.

She looked directly at Razzle with an almost imperceptible trace of respect and said in a voice bordering on kindness, "You are going to write a book."

But for Razzle there was no pretending. She'd seen that look on Sonia's face and there wasn't a way in the world she could unsee it—ever. She was dying to know what was in those cards to cause that kind of reaction but somehow, without knowing why, sensed she wasn't supposed to ask, and to be completely honest, part of her was scared shitless to find out.

"I think you may have made a mistake?" doubted Razzle, unsure about much of anything in that instant.

Sonia leaned forward, staring deep into Razzle Dazzle's eyes, and replied in a voice filled with unwavering self-assurance and an intensity of conviction that left no room for a single shred of doubt, *"If I see it, it will happen."*

"B-b-but I'm not a writer..." mumbled the thunderstruck girl weakly, wishing with all her might that she was.

# CHAPTER 1

## RAZZLE DAZZLE AND THE BUTTERFLY OF BALANCE

Once upon a time, long before smart phones, reality TV and social media were invented, there stood an unlikely looking heroine wearing a big floppy hat and red go-go boots oscillating at a crossroad in *The Middle of Somewhere*. This wild haired, free spirit went by the name of Razzle Dazzle, and it was clear from the expression on her scrunched up face, that this gal was in a bit of a quandary.

At this juncture of her young life, Razzle was a clueless college graduate opting to wander the world doing whatever came her way instead of getting a "real job", which to her sounded like the biggest drag ever. Born under the traveling sign of Sagittarius, she naturally possessed a gypsy soul devoid—for the most part—of fear and prejudice, and was perfectly content flying by the seat of her pants, letting the wind blow her around from place to place, happily acting out her role as the champion of the underachievers.

Before graduating from college, she came up with the brilliant idea of supporting herself by winning the lottery. So one day Razzle wrote down the first six numbers that popped into her head, went down to the local convenience store and won. Now it wasn't a huge jackpot, mind you, but it was a tidy little sum for a girl who wanted to travel and live simply. She never told a soul, and got by stretching out her winnings and picking up cool jobs here and there so she looked legit. It was the perfect cover for the snoops who felt the need to know her business, and also for the ones who mattered, her peeps who were genuinely concerned about her well-being.

Lately, though, there was a little nagging voice causing her some angst, pressuring her to put her degree to good use and head back to *The Real World* to begin a socially acceptable career. However, she was doing her best to ignore it, at least until the money ran out.

Now albeit Razzle had a higher education, she wasn't exactly what you'd call a big thinker. She mindlessly cruised along doing her thing, taking life as it came without asking too many questions or getting too deep. She wasn't entirely sure what she believed in—herself mostly, she guessed—but in line with her mentally shallow nature, she wasn't even aware of why she thought that.

As for the rest of the big picture, she really couldn't say nor did she care much about finding out. Her lifestyle and lack of philosophy were working out for her just fine, thank you, and for reasons the oblivious vagabond never bothered to consider, no matter what kind of situation she found herself in, she always seemed to land on her feet. But sooner or later, fate has a funny way of booting your ass through a door, and even though Razzle hadn't seen it coming, that moment for her had just arrived.

So with hands resting on hips attached to a pair of long, skinny chicken legs, she cast her gaze over the signpost indicating her options. The arrow pointing to the left said CITY, the one pointing to the right said OCEAN, and the arrow pointing straight ahead said MOUNTAINS. And from the looks of things, it appeared that all were under equally uncertain consideration.

"Where am I?" she asked out loud. "I thought I knew my way. I thought I had it all figured out..."

"You are blocked," replied a woman's voice with an indistinguishable accent from out of thin air, causing Razzle to nearly jump out of her skin.

She whirled around, expecting to see the woman standing behind her, but strangely, there wasn't a soul in sight. Feeling a tad uneasy and a little creeped out, Razzle did her best to convince herself that her ears must be playing tricks on her. However, with discretion being the better part of valor, she chose to err on the side of caution and called out tentatively, "Hi! Is anybody there?"

"I am here, I am here, I am here!" came the same odd, unseen voice once again.

Razzle spun around for the second time, eyes wide, heart racing, only to find herself still completely alone. This was impossible! Where on earth was this woman?

Then, all at once, she realized the voice she'd heard had actually come from *over* her head. Gripping the top of her hat, she slowly looked up and hovering right above her was the most far-out looking butterfly she'd ever seen. It had black and white yin-yang wings, a human head with short, spiky blonde hair and piercing golden eyes eerily reminiscent of the mysterious psychic, Sonia, she'd met years ago. Razzle gaped as the butterfly floated down, suspending herself gracefully with perfect equilibrium, so she could speak with the girl face-to-face.

"Please allow me to introduce myself," said the butterfly in a very professional manner.

"I am The Butterfly of Balance, but you may refer to me as BB."

Razzle Dazzle stared stupefied at the little creature, attempting to process what was going on. Was she hallucinating? She loved kooky things and all, but this was really out there! She didn't do drugs so she knew it wasn't the result of any residual backlash, and the fact that she was questioning what was taking place led her to believe she still had the capacity to reason, which in turn must indicate she was sane. Right? Right. And although she was freaking out a weeny bit, she was also inexplicably drawn to the butterfly in a way she couldn't comprehend. So she figured, What the hell? Let's just go with it and see where it leads.

"Nice to meet you. I'm Razzle Dazzle, but you can call me RD," she introduced herself all casual-like, digging the butterfly's brevity of style, quickly hijacking it for herself and coining her alias.

"Hello, RD. It is a pleasure to make your acquaintance. I am here to let you know that the place you have reached is *Self*

*Doubt* and as I was saying, the reason you do not know which way to go is because you are blocked."

"What do you mean...I'm blocked?"

"You are stuck now, no? Hesitating to make a decision because somewhere along your path you inadvertently stopped trusting yourself and lost your inner balance," declared the butterfly, enlightening the girl on the cause of her dilemma.

Razzle's eyes crossed ever so slightly and she gave her head a quick shake to set herself straight again. "I'm sorry," she replied, "but I have no idea what you're talking about."

"Is it my accent?"

"No, no! Not at all! I love your accent! What I'm trying to say, is that I understood the words, I just don't get the *meaning*."

"Ohhhh. I apologize for the confusion. Please allow me to explain. You see, each one of us has multiple sides to our character and we need to try to balance all of these aspects of ourselves so we are in harmony. I am an expert at maintaining impeccable balance and am here to assist you with achieving yours."

"So you're basically here to help me get my shit together then?"

"Yes, I suppose that is correct, although there is no reason to be a potty mouth. If you do not mind, please try to clean up your act when you are talking to me," requested the butterfly politely but firmly.

"Oh! I'm sorry! It pops out like that sometimes. Please forgive me if I offended you. I certainly didn't mean to." And she didn't. It was never Razzle's intention to be vulgar. She just talked that way because she felt that throwing in a cuss word here and there really and truly jazzed up a conversation and it was just her natural way of speaking.

"No offense taken, but you should be mindful of the words you use. It matters, you know."

Really? questioned Razzle silently, filing that warning away for future reference. She had a feeling it might mean something more to her one day, but for now she was just getting a kick out of having a real live conversation with a butterfly. Even if said butterfly was a little uptight and never used contractions.

"So what do I have to do to find my balance again?" asked Razzle, getting back to business.

"You must start to meditate."

*"Meditate?"* Razzle grimaced wanting to puke, envisioning a bunch of oddballs zoning out on a beach somewhere. Joining that group of weirdos didn't appeal to her in any way, shape or form, but she'd already ruffled BB's wings once and didn't want to risk a second violation by shooting her down. So deciding it would be wise to just play along, she asked in her best in-authentic interested voice, "How do I do that? I've never done it before."

"You do not need to do anything special. Just find a quiet place, sit down and breathe through your groin."

"*What???*" blurted Razzle, unable to control herself from automatically picturing a totally disgusting mental image.

"Just focus your attention on breathing from your groin area instead of your lungs," instructed the ever-tolerant BB, ignoring the juvenile obnoxious outburst. "That is really the proper method of breathing. Do not worry about it. Do what is comfortable for you and simply quiet your mind."

And with the wave of a yin-yang wing, the little creature flew off, leaving a dazed and confused newly self-christened RD gazing blankly at the space where The Butterfly of Balance had been seconds before, asking herself, "Did a butterfly with spiky blond hair really just tell me to breathe through my coochie cat?

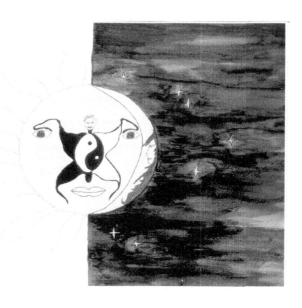

## CHAPTER 2

## HELLO, MEDITATION!

Well this is certainly one for the you-can't-make-this-shit-up-file, thought Razzle.

But as nutso as it definitely was, the truth of the matter remained that she still had no inkling about which road to take and decided she had nothing to lose by taking the trippy little butterfly's advice.

"Why the hell not?" She said out loud, shrugging her shoulders, and then immediately covering her mouth with her hands like a little kid. "I mean, why the *heck* not?" she corrected herself post haste, then zeroed in on a wooded area just off the road side that looked like a pretty good spot to give the meditation thing a whirl. She traipsed around until she found a place to her liking with a secluded thicket providing sufficient privacy from any potential prying eyes and pulled her sarong out of her bag, spreading it across the ground in preparation for the big event.

Now Razzle's "bag" was actually a little homemade jobby consisting of a tree branch about two feet long with an orange bandana tied into a pouch hanging from the end of it where she kept her essentials. It was her very own design—even though she'd pirated the idea from The Fool in the tarot cards—and she called this original accessory the Hobo Carrying Case. However, just like she abbreviated her name after meeting The

Butterfly of Balance, she decided here and now that it would forevermore be known as her "HCC".

So with that settled, Razzle took a seat, arranging herself in what she deemed to be an appropriate meditation position. Copycatting the Buddha statues she'd seen in her travels, she crossed her legs Indian-style, resting her upturned palms in her lap. Then, seeing as the butterfly had said there was no set technique, she chose to do what she did best—wing it!

"Okay, here goes..." she said, checking first over both shoulders to make sure the coast was clear and closed her eyes. "Now, breathe through my beaver...Oops! I mean *groin.*"

She imagined taking in air through her "groin" like she'd been told, bringing it up through her core, past her lungs and expelling it out her mouth (she was a mouth breather) and then back again, moving it in a big circle, over and over. She was relieved at how much easier it was then she'd thought it was going to be and continued breathing as BB had instructed, falling into a streamlined little groove.

"Next," she said to herself, "quiet my mind." And immediately her brain was all over the place, going a million miles an hour like a runaway train. She stopped everything she was doing, snapping open her eyes in total annoyance.

"Damn it!" she cursed, frustrated with herself and realizing right away she'd slipped again. "Ahhhhhhh!" she growled, now even more irritated with her mounting incompetence. Man, censorship was tough! But she wasn't giving up on this yet, and one way or another, she was getting this stupid meditation right.

Refusing to be thwarted, Razzle pondered for a minute and somewhere back in the recesses of her mind, remembered seeing a Tina Turner movie where Tina meditated. Didn't she say, *Om* when she did her thing? For some reason Razzle was pretty sure that she did, and elected to throw it into the mix and see what happened. So preparing herself for round two, she busted out her Buddha pose again.

"Carry on, soldier!" she declared, barking at herself. Then she checked again for intruders, closed her eyes and began her process for the second time. She got her breathing going and confidently said, *"Ommmmmmmm..."* dragging out the sound the way she'd heard it done in the movie. *"Ommmm..."* she repeated, saying it over and over, feeling the vibration of it in her ears and throat in a strange but cool way.

Razzle was so busy concentrating on what the *Om* was doing, that she was totally unaware that she'd stopped thinking about anything else except hearing and feeling it. Then, very naturally, she stopped saying *Om* and heard a low humming tone in her ears reminding her of the sound a boat motor makes when you've got your head underwater or the vibration of cicada songs filling the air.

It started out soft and gradually became stronger but not loud. Then, it faded away, and as it grew quiet again, she felt a weird sensation in her head, as if it was inflated with a type of energy of some sort. It felt kind of light and airy and was hard

11

to explain exactly, but something was definitely floating around in there that hadn't been there before.

Razzle sat still, waiting for whatever was supposed to happen next to happen, and finally heard a voice say, "FIND YOUR BALANCE."

"Holy shit!!!!!!!!!!!!!!!"

Freaking out, Razzle jumped up like someone had just lit a stick of dynamite underneath her, certain she was about to have a heart attack and drop dead in the bushes where no one would ever find her until she was nothing but bones.

"BB!" she yelled, super pissed and positive the butterfly was messing with her. "BB, I know you're there!" she called again scanning the sky.

But the butterfly wasn't around. In fact, no one was there at all except for Razzle herself. And then it sank in. The reason she couldn't see anybody was because it wasn't any *body* who'd spoken at all! It wasn't a normal voice belonging to a person... It was a *thought-voice* not a *voice-voice*—not a *real* voice!

"Whoa..." said Razzle, trying to wrap her head around what just went down. "Did I just make that up?"

She was beginning to scare herself a bit, but she'd be a big fat liar if she didn't admit to finding the whole thing utterly fascinating! It was like being sucked in by some blockbuster movie that she couldn't possibly tear herself away from, even if she tried. And honestly, she was way more interested in the idea that she might *not* be losing it and this *was* really happening than the fear of being committed.

So Razzle sat straight back down, waiting until she managed to get her heart rate under a thousand beats a minute and assumed the position. She launched into her routine again and the same things happened in the same way, and she heard *the thought voice* say, "LET GO OF THE THINGS THAT WEIGH YOU DOWN."

And as soon as she heard the words, she saw a picture in her head of her hand releasing a bunch of balloons. Inside the balloons were her demons—insecurity, lack of confidence, doubt, pressure to conform—and as she watched the balloons drifting upward, the strings attached to each one fluttering in the wind, she literally felt a huge weight lift from her body and float away with the balloons as they drifted out of sight.

Razzle's eyes opened in shock, completely floored by the unbelievable weirdness. "Far-out," was all she could manage to whisper, sitting there letting everything sink in. And when she could finally settle down, she began trying to rationalize it.

Okay, she reasoned as calmly as she could, Let's just say for argument's sake that the first time I heard *the thought voice,* it's possible it *may* have been my imagination...But to hear it *twice????* Come on! There's absolutely no way—no effing way—on the planet that I could be concocting this entire thing up on my own.

"This is so cool!!!!!!! And it's *real!!!!!!!!!!!*"

Razzle immediately grabbed her HCC, whipped out her notebook and pen and began scribbling furiously. This was off-the-hook craziness and she wasn't going to risk forgetting a single detail of it! And even though she had no idea what just happened, the clueless wonder was switched on enough to figure out that she'd just opened a door that was about to lead her on a whole new adventure!

## CHAPTER 3

## THE VOICE THAT ISN'T A VOICE

Just as Razzle finished writing the last word of her wild experience, she lifted her head and found herself staring into the hypnotic golden eyes of The Butterfly of Balance. "Well, it appears you have not gotten very far."

"BB! Meditation is awesome!"

BB chuckled at the girl's exuberance. "I am pleased you were successful with connecting with The Source."

"The Source? What does that mean?"

"It is THE VOICE THAT ISN'T A VOICE. You heard it, did you not?"

"Yes! That's exactly what I heard! THE VOICE THAT ISN'T A VOICE!" exclaimed Razzle, thrilled to be calling it by its appropriate name. "And it told me to find my balance and let go of the things that weigh me down, and I did! I let go of all the junk that stresses me out, and I feel so much lighter! Then I wrote everything in my notebook, so I wouldn't forget it. I even wrote about you!"

"Ahhhh. Very good, RD. Now you are well on your way to becoming unblocked. You are ready to continue your journey."

"What? Wait a minute! Are you saying I'm still blocked?" bleated an incredulous Razzle Dazzle.

But how was that even possible? What about her stellar meditation performance? She'd heard THE VOICE, she felt lighter...Why wasn't she cured? Did that mean she was chronic? And just how was she supposed to continue her journey in this blocked and unbalanced condition? The poor girl was crestfallen at her failure.

Razzle's head was spinning, but she certainly didn't want the butterfly to know she was losing her shit. So in the most off-handed manner she could muster she asked, "But now what? How will I know which way to go?"

"You have to trust yourself. Most people do not trust themselves enough and go outside of themselves for answers. That is why so many individuals feel unhappy and powerless. But the truth is, you have all your answers within. Go to The Source for the solutions and trust the information you receive. Do not doubt yourself."

"But BB, if I go to The Source aren't I going outside of myself for answers? I thought you just said *I* have all the answers?"

"You are part of The Source; we all are. So when you communicate with THE VOICE THAT ISN'T A VOICE, in essence you are speaking with yourself."

"*Huh???* What are you saying? Listen BB, I'm sorry, but this is way over my head," moaned Razzle, pulling her floppy hat down and hiding her face with it.

"Hush now," soothed BB. "I will explain it to you."

Razzle released the brim of her hat so her face was visible again, displaying a relieved expression of cautious optimism, eagerly awaiting her tutelage.

"To begin, everything in the universe is made up of energy, and this energy cannot be created or destroyed, it only changes its form. Correct?"

"Yes..." agreed Razzle hesitantly, recalling the statement from some boring science class or other. She conjured up a memory of the solid-to liquid-to gas experiment, the relevance of which she completely dismissed at the time, wishing now she'd paid a little more attention.

"So right now," continued BB, "you are RD energy as a human being. However, one day you will die and your body will be gone but your energy, or spirit if you prefer, still remains. Your spirit—the energy of YOU—is part of The Source which is made up of all the energy which exists in the universe. Do you follow me so far?"

"I guess so..." responded Razzle, her glassy eyes suggesting otherwise. "It makes sense—sort of—but this stuff is so *deep.* I've just never thought about anything like this before. I mean I get it—at least I'm pretty sure I do—it's just really *heavy* is all."

"Indeed it is, but you must continue focusing on what I am saying if you wish to help yourself. I can give you information but if you do not act on it, then it is useless."

"I promise I'm focusing," swore Razzle, legitimately attempting to concentrate.

"Now, what you must comprehend is that the energy of YOU is much larger than RD as human energy. It resides in other forms and these alternate forms of YOU exist all at once. So during meditation you are communicating with various selves as well as with other energy which comprises The Source, and if you and your alternate selves exist all at once, this means that time as you know it is an illusion."

The butterfly paused there for a minute, gauging the girl who looked like she'd just been shot out of a cannon. But nevertheless, annihilated brain or not, BB determined it essential to press forward.

"Consider the earth turning on its axis. There is no beginning and no end to its rotation; it is forever continuous. It is the same with time. There is no beginning, no ending. It is, was, and always will be infinite. Its concept has been created to simplify the idea for human beings so they perceive life in a linear, sequential manner and is generally accepted without question to be fact. But time is actually an illusion. What *appears* to be is not what *is*."

"You've got to be kidding me, right? Just what the hell are you talking about? I've got a pretzel in my head!" wailed Razzle, clutching her head in her hands and squeezing it while BB waited patiently for her to finish throwing her little fit until she spoke again.

"Try to calm down and please stop cursing," she requested. "During our relationship I will tell you things that you will not understand right away. It is okay. You will remember them anyway, and one day you will say, 'Ah-ha! So *that* is what the BB meant!' and at that moment you will grasp it completely."

Razzle perked up after that announcement, even though her mind was still blown to smithereens.

"So does that mean we—you and I—aren't finished yet?" she asked, giddy at the thought of continuing to cruise along with "the BB" on this weird but wonderful whatever it was.

"Goodness, no! You still have a lot of work to do, RD."

Just how much was *a lot*? Razzle wondered silently, skeptical she'd be able to handle much more of this confounding material. But on the other hand, she was relieved to know she wouldn't be going solo with this stuff—at least for the time being anyway.

"So although you may still feel discombobulated, you must look on the bright side" instructed BB.

Razzle grinned. She loved bright sides!

"And what would that be?"

"Now you should understand that you have the ability to converse with THE VOICE THAT ISN'T A VOICE."

"Are you telling me I'm allowed to talk and ask questions and not just wait for it to speak to me?" asked Razzle intrigued, lighting up at the idea.

"Of course. But you must open your mind so you can receive information that comes in many different ways. You need to listen for THE VOICE THAT ISN'T A VOICE, but not only while meditating. Communication is everywhere. The universe is always speaking to you, helping you, and once you begin to hear it, it will lead you to your answers."

"I don't get it," said Razzle bluntly, tired of feigning understanding to disguise her lack of esoteric sophistication.

"I will make this very simple for you. Consider the song you like, *The Highwayman*."

Razzle was taken aback. How did BB know she liked that song?

"Why do you like it?"

She gaped like an idiot at the butterfly, shrugging her shoulders in reply, not saying a word but thinking to herself, Well duh....Because I do.

"And the answer is NOT, *Oh, I just do*," said BB, rocking and shocking Razzle straight to the bone, capturing her full and immediate attention. "There is a deeper reason for your affinity for that particular song. Listen to the words."

Then the butterfly proceeded to sing the verse by Johnny Cash in her unique accent:

*I'll fly a starship across the universe divide*

*And when I reach the other side*

*I'll find a place to rest my spirit if I can*

*Perhaps I may become a highwayman again*

*Or I may simply be a single drop of rain*

*But I will remain*

*And I'll be back again, and again, and again, and again...*

BB finished her serenade and stared expectantly at Razzle for a sign of recognition but received nothing of the sort.

"That, RD, is communication. But you will only hear it if you listen. The *reason* you like that song is because it speaks to you. It is part of what you believe about life. *It is your truth."*

"Ohhhh..." responded Razzle, a faint glimmer of awakening registering in her eyes.

"There are times when you need to understand the *reason* behind something. Knowing when to look for an explanation is part of finding your balance. You must learn to open your mind."

Razzle nodded her head up and down, "I'm starting to get the picture, BB, and I'm really going to work on that."

And she wasn't just saying it so she wouldn't feel like a fool either. She really *was* picking up on what the Butterfly of Balance was putting down...somewhat. But be that as it may, she was up to her eyeballs in profound, overwhelming mumbo jumbo and figured it was high time to have a far less strenuous conversation. So she decided to turn the tables on BB and get her to talk about herself for a change. Ah-ha!, thought Razzle smugly, let's see how she likes those apples!

"BB, there's something I'd like to ask you if you don't mind," began Razzle strategically.

"By all means."

"Not to switch the subject or anything, but if you're a butterfly, why do you have a human head?"

"Because the spirit of nature and the spirit of human beings are woven together in each and every living thing. There is no separation; they overlap."

Razzle stared dumbly at the butterfly, struggling to reply. "Uh, I see," she lied, watching BB fly away, sagging in mental defeat as her brilliant plan blew up all over her face. But like a good little defiant loser, her dejection quickly turned to anger.

"Just how in the HELL," she swore as loud as she could, "am I supposed to figure this SHIT,"—twice for good measure—"out?"

She was so twisted up she felt like crying, but instead she sat down on the ground, reached for her notebook and wrote:

*Trust yourself.*

*Go to The Source.*

*Open your mind.*

And when she looked at the words she'd just written, Razzle discovered herself unexpectedly inspired by a spark of confidence that had been absent for quite a while. Hey now!

Putting it into that perspective certainly cleared things up! If breaking BB's gibberish down to the basics was what she needed to do to decode what the unintelligible little creature was talking about, so be it! That's exactly what she'd do!

"Hooray for me!" whooped Razzle, basking in her own cleverness.

But just while she was busy patting herself on the back, she gasped and stopped short. It was as if someone had just walloped her over the head with a hammer as she heard the words of The Butterfly of Balance ringing in her ears, "*You have all your answers.*"

## CHAPTER 4

## A LIST OF LITTLE HAPPINESSES

"Good grief!" muttered Razzle Dazzle shaking her head in a mutual combination of awe and disbelief at the beyond bizarre world she apparently now resided in.

Her brain felt like it had been kicked through the goal posts, and all she wanted to do was hit the closest bar and take the edge off her weary mind, but it was time to stop lollygagging around and make a move. The sun was high overhead and the morning had long since gone, but before getting back on the road she wanted to test out BB's claim and have a chat with THE VOICE THAT ISN'T A VOICE and see if she could get it to tell her which way to go. And besides, in her opinion the meditation was the grooviest part of all this madness and she was hoping to top the balloon trick from earlier!

So organizing herself once again on her sarong, she closed her eyes and went into her routine and it wasn't long before she heard the tone in her ears. When the sound stopped, she felt the funny feeling energy in her head, which was her cue to speak.

"Hello," she said. "Thank you for coming."

Then she actually felt THE VOICE THAT ISN'T A VOICE smile and heard, "Of course," which made Razzle smile, too.

This was great! BB was right! She *could* have a conversation! Then she thought-spoke, "I'm not sure which road to take. Can you please help me decide?"

She waited patiently then heard, "GO TO THE THINGS YOU ARE DRAWN TO. THERE IS NO RIGHT OR WRONG. FOLLOW THE DRAW. JOY IS THE FUEL OF LIFE."

Razzle remained still until the sensation in her head had gone and opened her eyes. "Wow…" she breathed. "Incredible!"

She sat for a second, digesting what just happened, then reached for her notebook and wrote it all down, elated over the success of the session. That's to say she was all pumped up until a little seed of doubt bordering on panic appeared in her mind causing her to ask out loud, "Am I psycho?"

And just as Razzle's looming thoughts of impending insanity began spiraling out of control, she heard the beating of little wings coming her way. BB swooped down, took one glance at Razzle and said, "Uh-oh. You do not look so good."

"That's because I'm afraid I'm losing the plot! What if I'm delusional and none of this is real? I mean, it seems real, and I'm sure I'm incapable of making this outrageous story up all on my own, and I swear I heard THE VOICE THAT ISN'T A VOICE…But oh my God! What if I didn't? And what about you? Butterflies don't talk! YOU can't possibly be real! Somebody help me!"

BB flew as close to the ranting girl's face as she could get and smacked it with her wings with all her might. "Owwwww!" shrieked Razzle, cupping her burning cheek in her hand, floored by the power of the tiny butterfly.

"Pull yourself together, please," ordered BB rather sternly, taking control of the situation.

Appalled at herself for behaving like a raving lunatic reduced to being bitch-slapped by a butterfly, Razzle composed herself. Feeling completely humiliated, she cast her eyes at the ground and took a couple of deep breaths.

"BB, I'm so sorry. Please forgive me. I'm just scared I've flipped my lid and none of this is really happening."

"Yet here we are, you and I," replied the calming voice of reason. "Do not doubt or second guess the information you are receiving. Believe what is happening and trust yourself."

"But it's so...*abnormal.* I feel like there's something wrong with me."

"There is. You have gone from someone who thought about nothing to someone who is thinking too much. You must find your balance."

And Razzle could see straight away that the butterfly was a hundred percent correct. No wonder she was all screwed up! She was overthinking all of this! She needed to get back to her old self and just enjoy this deviancy for what it was—whatever it was. Who cares if she was going insane? If that turned out to be true, then at least insanity was interesting!

"Thank you, BB. You're absolutely right. And from now on, I'm going to trust what's happening and find my balance, and I promise not to be a maniac anymore."

"Very good then. Now we will move forward," announced BB, getting back to business. "Have you made your decision on which road you will take?"

Razzle glanced at her notebook to refresh her memory and repeated what THE VOICE THAT ISN'T A VOICE had said.

"Excellent. This makes it very easy for you to choose then, does it not?"

"Well, yes I guess so...No, not really..." sputtered Razzle.

"Why are you so wish-washy?"

"Because it's cryptic, and I'm not entirely sure what it means. I'm embarrassed because I should be catching on a lot quicker, and I feel like a knucklehead."

"Absorption can take time. I promise this will not always be confusing for you, and someday you will no longer need me whispering in your ear," smiled BB reassuringly.

"You are trying too hard to make things happen, and all you are doing is continuing to block yourself. Do not put pressure on yourself. You need to become free flowing. Stop searching and let it come."

"I'll try," sighed Razzle half-heartedly, still bewildered by what BB was talking about most of the time.

"Just take one step at a time. Do not get too far out in front. Each step will lead you somewhere. The universe wants you to succeed. You are not alone."

"I will help you," said the butterfly with compassion. "You heard, *joy is the fuel of life* and *go to the things you are drawn to*, correct?"

"Yes."

"Okay. What do these words mean to you?"

"I should do things that make me happy."

"Excellent! You see? It is not so difficult at all. If something can be made simple, RD, do not make it complicated."

"For once, I understand *that* completely!" grinned Razzle, ecstatic to finally be fathoming one of BB's explanations.

BB laughed too, glad to see the girl enjoying herself once again, and continued elaborating. "So as you know already, you are made up of energy particles. You must keep those particles smiling. Think of them as your children—keep them happy. It is the sum of the little happinesses that make up the whole."

"So that means all the little things that make me happy create my total happiness?"

"Precisely."

"That makes sense," said Razzle, nodding her head in understanding.

"Perhaps it would be helpful if you made a list of those things—your little happinesses. Of course you would never be able to think of everything, and naturally you have yet to experience all the joys you will experience in your lifetime. But if you write down a few, it will assist with reminding you— especially when you may need a little pick-me-up somewhere down the road." And with those parting words of wisdom, the little butterfly was gone again.

"What a great idea! I love that idea!" Razzle shouted after the butterfly. "Good-bye, BB! Thanks again!"

Then she picked up her pen and wrote in her notebook:

## My List of Little Happinesses

-the sound of crashing waves

-a group of pelicans flying in formation

-seeing the sun rise over the water

-the taste of a perfectly made gin and tonic

That was a pretty good list, she decided, looking over it and feeling happy just thinking about all those things. Then it suddenly dawned on her...she knew *exactly* where she was going!

Razzle quickly gathered up her notebook and pen, folded her sarong into an itsy-bitsy square, and stuffed all of it into her HCC. Then she made her way back to the crossroad where the whole production began, and with total conviction turned right and began marching toward the ocean.

# CHAPTER 5

## NOT ALL WHO WANDER ARE LOST

Razzle clip-clopped for hours along the road leading to the ocean, immersing herself inside the bubble of lunacy encircling her morning, the rhythm of the swinging bandana pouch of her HCC keeping time with her steps. Deep in thought, she never heard the approaching car until it had already sped past her and was grinding to a screeching halt about fifty feet in front of her, startling her out of her reverie.

"Sweet Jesus!" she cried, jumping back off the road and watching as the white stretch limousine began inching its way backwards toward her. It stopped right alongside her, so close Razzle could see her reflection staring back at her from the black tinted glass of the passenger window. Then she heard the hum of the window descending, and a cloud of skunky smelling smoke came pouring out of the car, enveloping her from head to toe.

When the smoke cleared, Razzle found herself eye-to-bloodshot eye with the driver of the vehicle. He was leaning across the passenger seat grinning at her like a Cheshire Cat, dressed from top to tails in full chauffeur attire, including the white gloves. He tipped his hat and said "Aloha, little sister! Care for a ride?"

Before Razzle could respond, the back window came down and a long skinny arm appeared, thrusting a glass toward

Razzle. "Margarita on the rocks, no salt?" offered a hospitable female voice.

Completely taken off guard, Razzle stared open-mouthed for a second before managing to answer, "Wow, that's awfully tempting…"

And it was! Damn, she wanted that margarita! But even she wasn't game enough to risk that. "But I think I'll have to pass. I appreciate it, though."

"Suit yourself," said the skinny arm, snatching the cocktail back inside the limo and vanishing behind the glass of the closing window, leaving Razzle free to turn her attention back to the patiently waiting stoned chauffeur, whose head was now hanging out the window.

"Does that go for the lift, too?"

Razzle smiled politely, not sure what to make of him or the margarita swilling passenger in the back seat. "Yeah, you know, thanks so much, but I really need the exercise."

The chauffeur let out a howl of laughter at the ridiculousness of the lame excuse, but graciously let her off the hook. "No problemo, little sister," he said. "See you somewhere down the road," he remarked casually, throwing Razzle a wink and withdrawing back into the car. Then he grinned his grin, flashed her the peace sign and put the limo in gear.

As he slowly pulled away, she noticed a bumper sticker extending across the entire length of the tail end that said, *Not All Who Wander Are Lost*. Something about the slogan struck her, but before she could even think twice, the chauffeur floored it and was off, charging down the road at the speed of light.

Razzle watched until the car was out of sight, amazed again by the ongoing weirdness of the day. She shook her head, clearing out the fast and furious incident that already seemed like a dream, and resumed walking.

"Not all who wander are lost," she said out loud, repeating the slogan on the bumper sticker. Hmmm...she dug that a lot, totally identifying with the statement, thinking the next time some condescending "adult" told her they hoped she found what she was looking for with all her traveling, blah, blah, blah..., guess what she was going to respond?

"Not all who wander are lost." Ha! She loved it!

Feeling empowered by the sentiment and honoring the hunger pangs poking at her belly, she picked up her pace, heading straight for a roadside diner she spied off in the distance. She reached the ram-shackled little building in no time, and although the sign out front was missing so many letters that the name of the place was indecipherable, the parking lot was full, and Razzle strode on in.

The diner was packed, save for the lone empty seat at the counter next to the cash register, where she plopped down, starving. An elderly waitress with a beehive hairdo and cat's eye glasses smiled at her and slapped a menu face-down in front of her. As Razzle was flipping it over to have a look, she happened to glance out the front window just in time to see a familiar white limo take a hard left into the parking lot, spraying gravel all over the place.

The next thing she knew, the whack-a-doodle chauffeur exited the still-moving vehicle and stumbled across the parking lot, blasting through the door of the little diner with arms extended over his head in victory.

The diner erupted in a chorus of cheers. "James!" cried the patrons in unison.

"Hey, hey, hey!" grinned the chauffeur, high-fiving his way around the room like a celebrity. When he got to Razzle, he bowed deeply, tipping his hat, giving her a knowing wink with his electric blue, laser-beam bloodshot eye.

"Aloha once again, little sister," he purred.

Razzle was speechless. She sat there stunned at the repulsive, yet oddly magnetic character whose presence was commanding everyone's complete attention.

Just then the elderly waitress appeared from the kitchen carrying a stack of to-go boxes, her face glowing with pride. She set them down in front of Razzle and leaned across the counter, giving James a big kiss.

"Here you go, Sonny Boy! It's all there. I'll just add it to your tab. Excellent dismount, by the way."

"Thanks, Mommasita! And here's a token of appreciation from the girls," said James the chauffeur, handing his apparent mother a wad of hundred dollar bills, squeezing her hand affectionately and grabbing the boxes.

"Give them my love!"

James blew the waitress a kiss, curtsied to his admiring crowd, and charged out the door of the little diner as fast as he'd come in. Razzle watched out the window as the limo's rear window came down and James passed the boxes through, unable to catch any glimpse at all of the passengers. Then, he jumped in behind the wheel, laid on the horn and peeled out of the parking lot, speeding off down the road again like a bat out of hell.

Absolutely unreal, marveled Razzle, entranced by the cloud of dust in the parking lot, the spectacle of James imprinted in her mind. As the image faded, Razzle returned her focus back to her hunger, absently flipping the down-turned menu right way 'round. She stared at its cover, steadying herself to keep from falling off her stool as she read, *Welcome to the Somewhere Down the Road Diner*—the parting words of her first encounter with James the chauffeur blaring in her head.

Then she heard a voice coming in from what seemed to be a million miles away saying, "What'll it be hon? I recommend the PB & J."

NOt ALL
WHO WANDER
ARE LOST...

## CHAPTER 6

## THE SPIRIT OF THE SUNFLOWER

After finishing a rather subdued but satisfying lunch in the wake of Hurricane James, Razzle was back on the road, grateful for the opportunity to breathe the air and clear her head. She marched along replaying the day's absurdities over and over again, and the only thing she was absolutely sure about was that she wasn't sure about anything.

She was still struggling with the idea that maybe she'd dreamt the entire episode up just like Dorothy in *The Wizard of Oz*. But she was also aware that sometimes things happened in this world that you just couldn't explain, and all you could do when they crossed your path was roll with it.

So with the daylight hours beginning to fade into evening, Razzle found herself at the crest of a hill looking down at a field full of sunflowers glowing majestically in the light of the sinking sun, and a smile spread across her face, beaming almost as brightly as the vision in front of her. She took off galloping down the hill to get a closer look and was immediately swallowed up by hundreds of huge, yellow-faced flowers, surrounded on both sides of the road as far as the eye could see. Razzle stood there for a moment in her own little world, admiring the beauty.

It's time for a break, thought Razzle, feeling an overwhelming sense of peace among the flowers. She waded deeper into the field, navigating her way through a maze of green stems, and pulled out her sarong and to-go sandwich from *The Somewhere Down the Road Diner* and proceeded to have herself a little picnic.

While Razzle sat munching her second yummy PB & J of the day, she kept a lookout for BB, half expecting her to make an appearance, and was a little let down when the quirky little butterfly failed to show up. But she got over her disappointment quickly, allowing the bedazzling sunflowers and sounds of nature to provide the entertainment instead.

When she was done eating, she decided to do a quick check-in with THE VOICE THAT ISN'T A VOICE to see what it had to say, but then stopped herself. What if she was over-doing this meditation thing and THE VOICE got sick of her shenanigans and stopped talking to her? She certainly didn't want to act like a stalker and chase the poor VOICE down every chance she got, did she? Just how would she like it if someone hassled her like that?

After a bit of back and forth, Razzle finally concluded that none of that crap mattered and vowed to keep her promise to herself and not overthink things. All she knew was that she found it cool as hell to be communicating with something that wasn't precisely human and came from who knows where, wondering for a second if maybe it was alien. "Well, why couldn't it be?" she asked herself. Anyway, it didn't make any difference. She just thought it was awesome.

So, she went ahead and set herself up, going through the now familiar routine, and predictably enough heard the tone deep in her ears, but for whatever reason it sounded different in pitch this time than it had before. And although Razzle noticed the difference, she didn't let it distract her. She stayed focused and eventually felt the lightness in her head, but that wasn't the same either. It felt very warm, like sunshine, and it also felt...happy. Actually, it was much stronger than happy—it was *joy*. And this particular energy seemed very, very familiar.

"Hello" Razzle said silently.

"Hi!" answered an equally silent sing-song voice.

"You're different from the usual VOICE, but I swear I know you somehow. Have we met before?" asked Razzle, knowing it was impossible but also believing at the same time that it wasn't.

"I'm The Spirit of the Sunflower and yes, we've met. Don't you recognize me?"

"Michelle!? Michelle is that you?????"

Razzle was stunned. She was positive it was her dear friend Michelle who'd recently passed away very suddenly, leaving behind a big hole in not only her life but in countless others' lives as well.

The two girls had clicked from the moment they'd met, immediately recognizing in the other the kindred spirit of the traveler. And although they were often apart, each one participating in their own separate escapades, neither time nor distance could break their bond. Michelle had understood what Razzle was all about and accepted her just the way she was, and a friend who gets you like that was hard to find, and—as Razzle had come to learn—was even harder to replace.

The new VOICE laughed, "It's me!"

"Oh my God! It *is* you! How are you?????? You're so...how do I say this? *Joy!* And I dig your new name! It's perfect for you! It's wild how even though you have a new identity, you're still the same YOU!"

"Hee, hee!" giggled her friend.

"Are you like my spirit guide or something?" asked Razzle, using a term she'd heard somewhere along the way but had no clue where it came from or what it meant.

"I don't know *what* I am...but it's sooo cool! Hee, hee!"

"It's wonderful to talk to you! And I mean that with all my heart!"

"Yeah. It's pretty great," agreed The Spirit of the Sunflower affectionately. "I was so happy when I saw you coming because I wanted you to know that I'm okay. Maybe you can tell the others."

"But do you think they'll believe me? They'll all think I'm nuts."

"They will believe you."

Razzle Dazzle wasn't so sure, but held her tongue, not wanting to ruin the incredible moment with her idiocy. Instead she asked, "So when you die, your energy really *does* carry on?"

"Yes. Your body's just a shell. You can leave it anytime but YOU are never gone. So here I am, and like I mentioned already, I'm not really sure what the deal is yet, but I'm just going with it, and I feel fantastic. I *am* joy, that's for certain, just like you said."

"Far out! But I guess I'm not really all that surprised. Maybe somehow I've always figured this is how it is."

"You're on a doozie of a ride right now, and you'll see there are a lot things that'll seem totally crazy and incomprehensible at first. But as you go along, you'll realize you've known them to be true—deep, deep down inside—you've always known. Now it's your job to dig and get to your truth, so you can move forward. You've got a lot of work to do!"

"You sound just like The Butterfly of Balance!"

"I adore her! And you should listen to her, Razzle," advised The Spirit of the Sunflower seriously. "She knows what she's talking about."

Then all at once, Razzle felt her friend's energy starting to fade. "I can feel you moving away."

"Yeah, I'm going..."

"Will you come back and talk to me again?" begged Razzle, crossing her fingers with her up-turned meditating palms.

"Oh, I'll be back...one way or another. We're connected, my little friend. So remember, you're never really alone—even when you're by yourself." And then the energy of The Spirit of the Sunflower was gone.

Razzle opened her eyes and a warm tear ran down her cheek. "We're connected," she repeated tilting her head back, looking up into the now darkening sky. She wasn't sure if it was real or her imagination, but she swore she could see the outline of The Spirit of the Sunflower against the backdrop of stars, dancing beneath a crescent moon, grooving back and forth to her own beautiful music, just swaying on her stem with her petals flowing wildly...laughing and laughing.

Razzle Dazzle smiled peacefully, lowering her head. Then she reached inside her HCC and pulled out her notebook and added:

*-speak to a special friend*

to her *List of Little Happinesses.*

# CHAPTER 7

## FLAMER THE TRAILBLAZER

"Holy crap! I just talked to a dead person!" realized Razzle, grasping the enormity of what just went down, the concept mind blowing yet comforting at the same time. The reality of the moment continued crashing, in and she wasn't too sure what to do with all of it. *Just what the hell was going on?* This stuff happened to fortune tellers, psychics and whatnot...not to *her!* This was insane!

Fortunately for Razzle she was able to put it all on the back burner as she suddenly noticed herself sitting in the middle of a sunflower field in the dark with no idea of where she was, where she was going, or where to spend the night. In one swift movement she was up and running back toward the road, stuffing her sarong into her HCC on the fly.

As luck would have it, she could see a bright orange light burning not too far up ahead that looked like flames from a campfire. Great, she thought, remembering overhearing some folks talking about a campground while she was having lunch at the diner. That must be it! I'll just head on over there and pitch up for the evening.

She scurried along the road toward the fire which was providing impressive visibility considering its distance between where she was and the blackness now engulfing her. When she got closer, Razzle called out so she wouldn't startle anyone. "Hello! I'm just coming to join you if that's okay!"

She received no response in return, and even though she didn't want to be an unwelcome guest barging in like this, she knew the intrusion was necessary and tiptoed up anyway. She stood alone in front of the roaring fire, puzzled by the unattended flames and the weird lack of a presence of a person, camping gear, or for that matter, anything at all. There was just a fire burning all by itself.

Razzle shrugged her shoulders, thinking it really was just par for the course at this point, and took out her trusty sarong from her HCC. But just as she was about to spread it out on the ground, she heard a sexually ambiguous voice drawl, "Well, hellllloooo there."

Razzle looked up hoping to see a camper, but as she expected, encountered nothing of the sort. "Here we go again," she sighed, acknowledging the salutation had indeed emerged from *inside* the fire.

Bracing herself for the inevitable crazy, she took a step forward gazing into the swirling heat, and within it, she saw a concentrated gathering of flames forming a kind of "body" belonging to what appeared to be a male of some persuasion sporting a goatee, a pair of designer sunglasses, a crown on his head and a feather boa around his neck. In one hand he gripped a martini, and in the other he held a long cigarette holder like the old movie stars used back in the day, a cigarette smoldering at the end of it. The fire alternated between taking a sip from his cocktail and a drag from his smoke.

"I'm Flamer the Trailblazer, baby! And let me tell you, honey, I...AM...HOT!" boomed the fire, larger than life, following up with a James Brown style howl like nobody's business. "WAH-OOOOOOW!"

"And just WHO might you be?" questioned the rather imperial sounding fire.

"I'm Razzle Dazzle, but you can call me RD," she answered feeling like it was Groundhog Day, marveling once again at how the madness simply refused to end.

"Hmmmmmm. That's quite an interesting name..." said Flamer, taking a swig from his martini, pondering its origin. "Is it a *stage* name?"

"A stage name?" asked Razzle warily, wondering what precisely he might be implying. "No. It's a nickname my dad gave me when I was a kid. It suits me better than my real name so I go by it."

"Oooooooooooohhhhhhh....Then it's an *assumed* name. So, in other words, you're hiding from yourself."

"What are you talking about? That's not true!" And as soon as the words were out of her mouth, Razzle instantly asked herself, "But is it?" Now that he'd said it out loud, she wasn't exactly sure. The thought had never crossed her mind before. This stupid fire was making her mad, getting in her head like that.

"Well my, my. Aren't we touchy, *Frazzle* Dazzle? Perhaps you'll want to consider that on a deeper level at another time, doll."

Then, suddenly changing his tone to one of the-hostess-with-the-mostess flair, the fire graciously said, "But for now, sweets, come on over and make yourself comfortable! And by the way, your bag is absolutely DIVINE! What is it? Prada, Gucci, Chanel?"

Razzle was totally confused by the manic fire's tactics. She'd never met anyone before who flip-flopped like that and didn't know what to make of it. But she was relieved they'd moved past her potential identity crises and onto a far more benign topic.

"Uh...it's my own design," she replied cautiously, laying her sarong down on the ground and taking a seat in front of the fire.

"Well, I think it's TERRIFIC! You should approach a major fashion house with that idea, honey. A mini version of it would be darling. Now tell me, what's a nice gal like you doing wandering around at this hour?"

"Well," began Razzle, grateful for the opportunity to recap the most recent segment of her journey, "I was talking to The Spirit of the Sunflower back in the big field, and by the time we'd wrapped it up it had already gotten dark. I wasn't sure what I was going to do and then—by coincidence—I saw your flames and came to see if I could crash here for the night."

"The Spirit of the Sunflower!" squealed the fire. "I just LOVE her! Everybody LOVES her! What's NOT to love about that wonderful ray of sunshine? Oh, and incidentally, there are NO coincidences AND Flamer the Trailblazer does NOT camp."

Razzle ignored the last remark completely, but happily agreed with him about The Spirit of the Sunflower. "Yes, she's very lovable indeed."

"She most certainly is, and she could definitely teach YOU a thing or two about love, little lady," spat Flamer with contempt, taking a monstrous gulp from his martini, reverting back to his former haughty disposition without warning.

Razzle glared at the fire. What's with this guy? Why was he coming at her again? He was like Dr. Jekyll and Mr. Hyde! She knew she was his guest and wanted to be nice, but this Flamer was really starting to piss her off.

"Just what do you mean by that?"

"You know EXACTLY what I mean. She was YOUR friend after all. She was just like you, blasting about all over the place having one adventure after the next—seeing, doing, meeting people from all walks of life, and just out-and-out making the most of her time on this great earth. Granted, there's nothing wrong with that, mind you. To each their own, I say! But there was one BIG difference between the two of you...SHE wasn't afraid of love!"

It had been a very long day and Razzle had put up with all of this schizophrenic Flamer and his self-righteous attitude that she could manage. Just who did he think he was judging her? She was tired, at the end of her patience, and she was done being polite.

She jumped up yelling at the fire, "I'm not afraid of love!"

"Are you married?"

"No!"

"Got a boyfriend?"

"No!"

"A girlfriend?"

"No! But so what? It's none of your business anyway! I like being by myself! What's wrong with that? I'm free as a bird and totally happy!"

She felt like sticking her tongue out at him, but knew she'd only look ridiculous and would just add fuel to the loser fire. *Up his!* she fumed, refusing to give him the satisfaction.

"You may THINK you're 'totally happy' as you say, but you're mistaken. In fact, Little Miss Independence, you're going to discover you've been mistaken about a great many things. But I will tell you this—and you'd be wise to write it down in that notebook of yours...."

*Hey! How did he know about her notebook?* wondered Razzle, furious at the invasion of her privacy, but also secretly impressed that he'd accessed that tidbit of seemingly in-accessible knowledge.

"The reason you can NOT possibly be 'totally happy' is because...THE SECRET TO TOTAL HAPPINESS IS...drumroll please...LOVE!"

Well that proclamation shut Razzle down right quick. She felt like a complete jackass and stood there mute, staring at the ground like a moron because somehow—and she wasn't quite sure how—she knew he was telling the truth.

Then Flamer the Trailblazer, who'd been smugly basking in his glory only moments before, saw himself as an utter schmuck while he watched the poor girl's reaction. The pitiful thing looked like she was about to burst into tears! Oh dear! He never meant to make her cry!

You see, although the fire didn't intend any harm, he had a pendulum-like personality that sometimes swung just a little too far to the side of scathing, and unfortunately, he'd past the point of no return by the time he realized he'd gone overboard. So now there was nothing he could do but survey the damage and backpedal at a frantic rate in an attempt to redeem himself.

"Oh please, PLEASE don't cry! I just couldn't BEAR it!" pleaded Flamer dramatically, sucking on his cigarette with a quivering hand. "Listen, Razz, I'm sorry if I was a bit brazen. I get carried away occasionally, that's all. I didn't mean to hurt your feelings, I truly didn't! But sometimes in life you just need someone to give it to you straight."

Razzle kept her head down. She could tell he felt bad but was still mad at him for being such a dickhead. Oops! She meant *jerk*—even if he was right. She was enjoying watching him squirm and let him go on for a bit longer.

"Come on now. Please don't be like that. I'm SOOOOO sorry! I REALLY am!"

"Oh, all right," sighed Razzle, lifting her head in tacit forgiveness, too tired to be angry anymore anyway.

"That's better now!" gushed Flamer, washing his instant relief down with another massive swallow of vodka. "Listen, doll, the point I was trying to make is that it's necessary to have another person in your life. A partner helps give us balance."

"I know you're right. It makes sense. It just never occurred to me before, and I feel like a big dope."

"Don't beat yourself up, hon. We're all here to learn."

"But Flamer, the problem is how do I make it happen? I've no idea how to be in love with someone or how to go about it. What if I'm not wired like that? What if I can't do it?"

"Sugar, if your heart's in the right place, you'll find a way to do ANYTHING."

"Razzle smiled at the fire, touched by his thoughtful words. "Awww...That's really sweet. Thank you for that."

Flamer burned a shade brighter with renewed pride, puffing out his glowing chest. "I only speak the truth. You've had a big day, doll. Now it's time to go to sleep."

And without putting up one word of a fuss, the worn out RD did as she was told. She bunched up her big floppy hat into a pillow, wrapped herself in her sarong and curled up by her new friend. She closed her eyes and dreamed of sitting on a balcony somewhere and sharing a swing chair with a guy whose face she couldn't see, watching a huge sun rising over crystal clear water.

The next morning Razzle woke up just in time to see the last embers of Flamer the Trailblazer turning into dusty ashes. She waited, listening for him to impart any final commentary or maybe belt out a theatrical James Brownesque farewell, but in the end, all she heard was a soft hiss, and he was gone.

Yowza! What a handful! she thought, grinning in spite of herself as she recalled her evening with the eccentric fire. But he was all right, ol' Flamer, conceded Razzle, grateful for his company, warmth, and most of all, his advice. But right now she was starving, stinky and desperately needed a coffee.

She stood up to check out the lay of the land in the light of day and couldn't believe her luck. Just there, steps away from where she'd slept, was a big sign that said *Campground — Full Facilities — Restaurant.* How about that? She'd actually spent the night right outside the campground and it happened to have everything she needed!

"Now isn't that a funny coincidence?"

And promptly, from somewhere inside her head she heard Flamer the Trailblazer reply, *I told you, doll...there are NO coincidences.*

Razzle cracked up. She knew it! There was no way in the world that guy was going away quietly! Still laughing, she gathered herself together, paraded through the entrance of the campground and headed for the showers.

# CHAPTER 8

## A LESSON IN MAGIC AND THE
## INTENTIONAL USE OF ENERGY

It was a brand new day, and a fresh, clean, high on caffeine Razzle Dazzle strolled out of the campground with a full belly and her HCC over her shoulder, ready to resume her trek to the ocean. But before shifting into high gear, she wanted to find a quiet place to sit so she could record her yet to be documented excitement, and of course, meditate.

With that thought in mind, she moseyed along until she saw a giant tree with a welcoming patch of grass underneath. She unpacked her HCC and began writing about meeting The Spirit of the Sunflower and Flamer the Trailblazer, remembering to include the significant messages and observations they'd given her to ponder. Finally, after she felt confident she'd covered everything, Razzle was ready for her meditation session.

She situated herself properly and began the procedure. Breathe, *"Om...."* breathe, *"Om..."* And when she heard the tone, she knew right away it was the original VOICE THAT ISN'T A VOICE.

"Thank you for coming," smiled Razzle.

THE VOICE THAT ISN'T A VOICE smiled back. "You are welcome."

"Can I ask you a question?"

"Certainly."

"How come I hear that tone in my ears whenever I begin meditating?"

"It is so you know that we are here."

"Oh. That makes sense," said Razzle, seeing the wisdom in it. "That's good." And she felt THE VOICE smile at her again, amused by her approval.

"But wait a second," she abruptly interjected. "Who's *we*?"

"We are a collective voice—a consciousness, if you will—speaking for countless energies and beings whose guidance is available to you at all times. It is enough for you to know that our assistance is of a benevolent nature, intending to provide you with clarity and purpose for achieving your personal empowerment and freedom."

Razzle had no idea what that meant, but the gist of it sounded positive which was fine enough for her, opting to fast forward past it so she could hurry up and get to the good stuff.

"Do you have any information for me?" she asked, totally digging the two-way conversation.

THE VOICE THAT ISN'T A VOICE didn't say anything at first, and Razzle was starting to think it really had gotten tired of her nonsense when she heard,

"TODAY IS THE MAGIC."

"THE MAGIC IS TODAY."

"YOUR GIFT IS YOUR ENERGY."

Then slowly the feeling in her head dissipated and she opened her eyes. She picked up her notebook and wrote down the words THE VOICE just said, then sat looking at them perplexed.

"What the heck am I supposed to do with that mumbo jumbo?"

"RD! I am so proud of you!"

"BB!"

Razzle lit up like a Christmas tree when she heard the butterfly's voice, genuinely delighted to be looking into her tiny friend's face again. "But why are you proud of me?"

"Because you said, *heck*!"

"Ahhhh, come on now...I'm not *that* bad!" laughed Razzle and BB together. "But I really have been making an effort to keep it clean...At least most of the time anyway!"

"That is good. It means you are learning how to retrain your brain. So what else have you been up to? I see you have chosen your path."

Razzle started filling BB in on all the happenings since their last meeting, catching her up to speed on her decision to take the ocean road and her encounters with The Spirit of the Sunflower and Flamer the Trailblazer. "And now I understand what you meant by me being human energy at this moment, but how I'll change form after death but still be ME! And also about the human spirit and the spirit of nature being the same because my friend—who was obviously a human when I knew her—is now a sunflower!"

Razzle babbled away, realizing that as she expressed herself, she honestly was comprehending the things she was telling BB about. She was actually *getting* this stuff!

"I am very impressed. You see? I told you it would become clear eventually. And as long as you do not put pressure on yourself, everything in your life will come to you in the same way, and you will continue to remove your blockages and become free flowing and balanced."

"Yahoo! There's hope for me yet!"

Razzle jumped up, doing a little victory dance with BB joining in, flipping and twisting, circling Razzle in true funky butterfly style. But in the middle of the celebration, Razzle got a flash of the latest info she'd received during meditation and the wind came out of her sails. She immediately pulled the plug on her fun and dejectedly plopped back onto her sarong, crushed to be right back at square one.

"I need your help again, BB!" implored Razzle.

But BB was still busy getting her groove on, whirling and twirling all over the place, totally unaware that she'd suddenly lost her dance partner to the black hole of despair. It took a moment for Razzle's cries to register, but once they did, she was right back on her game and ready for action, floating back down to join Razzle at her self-imposed lower level.

"I am here," she reassured her.

"BB, what does THE VOICE THAT ISN'T A VOICE mean by, *today is the magic, the magic is today,* and *your gift is your energy*?"

"It means that what you produce as the results of your efforts is what you do today. How you direct your energy today and the success that comes from it is the magic. There is no other time but now."

"Oh brother, here comes another round of pretzel head!"

"RD, please try to attempt a different perspective. I am doing my very best to clarify these things for you."

"I'm sorry," apologized Razzle, ashamed of herself. She knew it wasn't BB's fault she was a bonehead. She'd better watch herself or her mentor might tell her to stick it, and then she'd have to figure it all out on her own!

"Please continue, BB."

BB locked eyes with Razzle, measuring her sincerity, and when she was satisfied of its authenticity, resumed speaking.

"Your power is your ability to direct your energy. Your gift then is your energy. You must use it, direct it. When you focus your energy intentionally, you can do anything. Are you beginning to understand a little?"

"A little, I think," lied Razzle.

"What you also need to recognize is the word *magic* is an expression and not literal. In truth, there is no magic. Even though some of this will seem like it at times, it is not. It may be magical, but it is not magic. The energy of intention exists behind all of it."

Then the butterfly took a deep breath, peering at Razzle who was listening intently and said, "And just as you will direct your energy to enhance the greater good, there are others in the world who direct their energy for opposite purposes. But none of it is magic — it is all the intentional use of energy."

"What do you mean...I'll direct my energy to enhance the greater good?"

"That is something I cannot tell you. You must discover it on your own. But do not concern yourself with that. Stay in the moment. Do not speculate about the future. In due time you will receive confirmation."

"Listen, BB, I'm a bit baffled here. If I'm not supposed to concern myself with the future, then what am I supposed to do now?"

"For now you must concentrate on becoming free flowing. Do not stop the flow of all that is and all you are. You are all elements — earth, air, fire, water. You are a sunflower, a butterfly a flame, a fish — all at the same time. You have many spirits. You must allow each one to be itself unrestricted. Think of yourself as a jellyfish, without bones, and you can move in all directions. There are no limits. Your energy has total flexibility, and it is up to you to guide it. But you have to make the effort. This will not happen all by itself like in a movie. Direct your energy, and you are going to see you will achieve remarkable things."

Then as usual, The Butterfly of Balance flew off without warning as quickly as she'd appeared, leaving Razzle alone to untangle the big mess in her head.

She closed her eyes, saying, "Deep breaths, deep breaths, deep breaths..."

She knew it was early, but man, she could use a drink! And right then her *List of Little Happinesses* popped into her head and she saw the line that read, *the taste of a perfectly made gin and tonic*, and damned if she didn't feel better!

"Well what do ya know!" she said, cracking up, realizing how the mere thought of a refreshing cocktail could cheer her up. Sad really, but so what? It worked! That BB may do a number on my head, but she sure seems to know her stuff, she laughed, remembering the butterfly's prediction of using her list as a little pick-me-up.

And with that merry burst of momentum, Razzle Dazzle managed to get over her mental hump. She quickly scribbled the basics of her conversation with The Butterfly of Balance in her notebook and repacked her HCC. It was time to get back on the road!

## CHAPTER 9

## A Cute Bartender, the World's Best G&T and Anything is Possible

Since firing herself up with her imaginary cocktail, Razzle had been cruising along at a pretty steady clip most of the day, spending the hours sifting and muddling over the mishmash of information inundating her fragile mind. The majority of it still mystified her, but at least she'd moved past thinking it was all a figment of her imagination. Besides, she knew there wasn't a way in hell that she was creative enough to spin a tale like this all on her own. And, as a side note, she'd made the executive decision that cussing in her own personal thoughts and conversations was definitely allowed—she didn't care what BB had to say about it.

It was late afternoon and Razzle was noticing the size of her lengthening shadow meandering in front of her when she began sniffing the air. She smelled the ocean! She picked up the pace, feeling a light salty breeze blowing the closer she got to the water. Straining her eyes trying to catch a glimpse of the beach, she was just in time to see a synchronized squadron of pelicans soaring across the sky before disappearing into the shimmering mist enveloping the coast.

From that point on, Razzle's feet seemed to move with a mind of their own, her red go-go boots in charge of escorting her the rest of the way down the road to the boardwalk where she clomped along each wooden plank until she reached the beach. She kicked off her boots, flinging them into a nearby dune, and let her toes sink into the warm sand.

"Awesome!" she said, a huge smile eclipsing her face.

Razzle followed the sound of the crashing waves, invisible behind the maritime mist, her figure vanishing like a ghost only to reemerge in seconds on the other side of the white veil of haze where she found herself looking directly at the beautiful blue-green ocean. For some strange meteorological reason that she had no concept of, the fogginess completely evaporated along the shoreline leaving the air crystal clear while the world behind her seemingly disappeared behind its shroud. She looked down the beach and saw a shack with the words BEACH BAR in big block letters painted across it.

"Yippie!" she rejoiced, fist-pumping the air and running back through the misty veil to the dune to grab her boots. She turned and burned, making a beeline straight for the watering hole, tear-assing down the beach as if her life depended on it. She purposely slowed her roll right before getting there, so she could stroll up nonchalantly like a normal person.

The simple little place was nothing fancy, but it was absolutely perfect. It was entirely open air with wooden stools surrounding the bar, each one facing the water. The bar itself was deserted except for the bartender and his only customer— a rather rickety, old-looking, orange and white cat occupying the bar stool all the way at the end.

"This is so cool!" she said out loud, heading for the seat next to the kitty.

The cat eyeballed her suspiciously, clearly not appreciating her uninvited presence one iota. Razzle caught its vibe, actually envisioning it flipping her the middle claw in her mind, but she was way too happy to let it stop her. She smiled, sitting down beside it anyway, thinking maybe it was just shy around strangers. The cat responded by turning its entire body in the opposite direction, making sure its ass end was facing her way.

Right about then, as if on cue, the bartender sauntered over and stood in front of Razzle, watching the exchange with an amused look as the cat made it perfectly understood just what was what. And although she really was hoping to be friends with the cat, she was picking up what kitty was putting down, and Razzle fixed her attention instead on greeting the dude who was about to make her day.

"Hi! I just love this place!" she gushed, taking off her hat and setting it with the rest of her belongings on the empty seat next to her.

The bartender smiled but didn't say anything, causing Razzle to think he must be shy also, just like the cat, deciding it might be better to take her enthusiasm down a notch until they became better acquainted. "I'll have a gin and tonic, please," she requested with slightly less gusto than was in her heart, uttering the words she'd been dying to say since that morning, composed on the outside but jumping up and down on the inside. She couldn't believe it! She'd done it—she'd made it to the ocean and it was happy hour to boot!

"Would you like one, too?" Razzle offered the bartender. She hated drinking alone, and it would be way more fun sharing this moment with someone.

"Sure," he said agreeably, grabbing two martini glasses from the shelf. "We only serve drinks in martini glasses here," he told her, preempting any further discussion regarding his choice of glass, then commenced to mixing two Tanqueray and tonics, each with a squeeze of lemon.

*LEMON????!!!!!!!!!*

Razzle Dazzle watched in horror as the idiot bartender contaminated the beverage she'd been dreaming about all day, biting her tongue to keep from screaming out, "Why would you *DO* that??? Everybody knows you're supposed to use LIME!"

But she kept quiet, swallowing her anguish while wiping the look of distress from her face and pasting on a smile as the bartender set her drink down in front of her. He raised his glass, looked her square in the eyes and said, "Cheers."

She did the same, clinking her martini glass against his. "Cheers," she said, choking back her disappointment, thinking instead, *What nice eyes you have Mr. Cute Bartender.*

Then she lifted her tainted cocktail to her lips, cringing as she took the first sip...And her eyes flew open wide and her face lit up...*It was delicious!*

"This is the best gin and tonic I've ever had in my life!"

"It's the lemon," replied the bartender smiling matter-of-factly. "Thanks very much for the drink, by the way. My name is Wolf."

"Wolf?" repeated Razzle, not sure if she'd heard him correctly.

"Yes."

"Is that your first name or your last name?"

"Yes."

She waited for him to elaborate, but when she realized that was all she was getting out of Wolf, she jumped in, "I'm Razzle Dazzle but you can call me RD."

"So it looks like you have three names," observed the perceptive Wolf. "You humans sure like to complicate things."

"Yes," she replied deadpan in a lame attempt to imitate him.

But she couldn't keep a straight face and busted up laughing instead, loving his sense of humor—at least she thought it was supposed to be a joke, that *you humans* remark. Whatever. All she cared about right then was breaking the ice and was thrilled to see Wolf laughing right along with her, prompting her to notice his cuteness again and wondered if there was a Mrs. Wolf in the picture.

"So is this your cat?" she asked quickly, trying to keep things rolling.

"It's more like I'm his. This is his bar. I work for him." Then he pointed to an engraved silver plate attached to the back of the cat's barstool that said, *THE BOSS.*

"Oh, that's nice." Two days ago that might have freaked her out, but now she didn't even bat an eyelash. "I guess that's why he gave me the evil eye when I came in—probably prefers locals."

"He's okay once he gets to know you, especially if you speak Cat. Do you speak Cat?"

"Uh...no, I don't," she replied, unsure of what Cat really was but certain she'd never learned to speak it. "Do you?"

"I'm fluent."

"Good for you," she said, trying not to look like a doorknob.

"Anyway, if you come around more, you'll become friends. He's just not a real people person, if you know what I mean."

"Believe it or not, I actually do." And believe it or not, she actually did, thanks to BB.

Reveling in the moment, Razzle looked out at the ocean, slowly sipping the most perfectly made gin and tonic in the world and continued chatting up the cute bartender until she noticed something taking form in the sky over the water. She stopped talking mid-sentence, staring as a translucent glowing white arc with a barely visible gibbous moon behind it slowly appeared, stretching from the shoreline all the way out to the waves in the middle of the ocean.

"Whoa! Look at that!"

Razzle launched herself off her barstool, startling the cat napping beside her and went flying out to the beach to get a better look. Wolf came out to join her, and together they stood riveted by the spectacular phenomenon.

"It's a white rainbow," Wolf informed her.

"*A white rainbow?* There's no such thing," retorted Razzle, even though it was right in front of her.

"Yet there it is," said the bartender, stating the obvious.

White Rainbow JWS 1/10/14

And then Razzle swore she heard the raggedy orange and white cat hiss, "Anything is possible girl!" from his seat on the other side of the bar.

She turned around and saw him glaring at her through hooded eyes. She wasn't sure if she'd made that part up or not, but at this point those types of questionable occurrences had ceased to matter and she turned her attention back to the white rainbow, not giving the probable talking cat a second thought.

"It's amazing! I want to touch it!"

And she took off charging down the beach full steam ahead, bound and determined to catch herself the white rainbow. But try as she might, Razzle couldn't seem to be able to reach it. Just when she thought she had it, it would suddenly change position and move farther away. She chased after if for a while but finally gave up, deciding that it really was enough just to look. She didn't need to walk through it to feel it's power or understand its meaning...Anything is possible. Just because you don't know something exists doesn't mean it doesn't.

BB was right, thought Razzle, communication is every-where—and this message was coming in loud and clear and she knew she'd never forget it. Somehow she was aware that this moment was important, though she couldn't put her finger on why she thought so. Then once again, she heard voice of The Butterfly of Balance echoing in her ears, *Trust the information you are receiving.*

"Wild..." said Razzle to the white rainbow, shaking her head in wonder. Then she turned around and ran back to the bar.

Huffing and puffing, Razzle threw herself onto her barstool a parched, hot mess. She collapsed in her seat, taking a giant gulp from her cocktail, expecting it to be completely watered down. But to her surprise, Wolf—the cute *and* thoughtful bartender—had been nice enough to freshen it up for her while she was away chasing the white rainbow. What a guy!

He stood there watching her, shaking his head and laughing. "You can't catch it."

"But why not?"

"You just can't. It doesn't work like that."

"Oh, well..." shrugged Razzle, honestly not minding a bit. "That's all right. It's still one of the most extraordinary things I've ever seen." And she watched the white rainbow until the light grew dim and it faded away, understanding there were times when it was okay not to look for a reason, that sometimes it was fine to accept something just as it was.

Razzle finished her drink, deciding that after last night's episode, she better not take any chances this evening. She needed to get herself some food and a place to stay, and she wasn't going to wait until it was pitch black out there again to do it.

"I've got to get going, Wolf. I need to settle up."

"It's on the house," he said, nodding his head toward the omnipresent cat who'd resumed napping after being so rudely interrupted earlier.

"Thank you so much. That's very kind of you," Razzle said to the cat.

The Boss opened one eye in acknowledgement and immediately went back to his business. Well, thought Razzle feeling flattered, he must have warmed up to me at least a little for him to pick up my tab! Then she put her hat back on her head, pulled on her boots and grabbed her HCC, confident Wolf could point her in the right direction. Bartenders were always in the know.

"Hey Wolf, is there somewhere close by where I can grab some food and stay the night?"

"There's a place that's a few minutes walk up the beach from here with rooms and a restaurant. You're lucky. It's off-season, so it'll be wide open."

"Perfect!" She loved it when a plan came together!

Razzle was just about to say good-bye to Wolf when he threw her a curveball, catching her completely off-guard. "Maybe you'd like to come run the bar with me for the season. Things will be getting busy here in a month or so and I could use the help."

Well the girl who'd been such a chatterbox since the minute she'd walked in, suddenly found herself at a loss for words. She hadn't seen that one coming and was totally tongue-tied. All she managed to come out with was a flustered sounding, "B-b-but what about The Boss?"

"It was his idea," Wolf informed her, handing her a business card that said, *The Water's Edge Beach Bar.* "Think about it and let me know."

"I will," said Razzle, regaining her composure and smiling brightly. "It was great meeting you!"

"You as well."

She looked down at the sleeping cat and was about to say good-bye to him too but changed her mind. Better quit while I'm ahead, she thought, and started to walk away. But before she did, she looked back over her shoulder, emboldened by her buzz, and said to Wolf, "By the way, you make a great drink."

Wolf just smiled, nodded his head and replied, "Nice boots," raising his eyebrows in appreciation and flashing her some unusually pointy looking teeth.

Blushing from head to toe, Razzle sashayed out of *The Water's Edge Beach Bar,* red go-go boots and all.

# CHAPTER 10

## TO THINE OWN SELF BE TRUE

Five minutes later, Razzle was standing in front of the reception desk, taking the key to her room from the hand of the super friendly girl checking her in. She figured that she and the receptionist were around the same age, and although they'd never met before, there was something about the girl that made her feel comfortable in a way she just wasn't able to put her finger on.

"You must have a sixth sense, showing up here now. After tomorrow we close everything down, and it's like a ghost town around here while we take a breather before season starts."

"Well I'd say it's a coincidence, but since there aren't any, I guess it was just meant to be!" replied Razzle.

"You got that right, sister!" laughed the receptionist. "Now you better hurry. Dinner's almost over, and you don't want to miss it. It's delicious, and I should know because I'm the chef here also! Hee-hee!"

Razzle laughed too, delighted by the charming girl. She thanked her, and prudently taking her advice, headed straight to the restaurant where her meal turned out to be as tasty as promised. She enjoyed every last morsel, pairing each bite with an equally scrumptious sip of her favorite wine—a lovely French rose`. And after sufficiently stuffing her face, Razzle waddled away like a little piggy to find room #1010, following the signs until she was standing on the porch of her very-own-for-the-night beach bungalow sitting smack dab in the sand, just steps from the water.

What more could she want? This was her new most favorite place on the whole entire planet! She was spending the night on the beach with the ocean air blowing through her open windows! She knew she was being a cornball, but it really felt like a dream come true.

After getting cleaned up and settling in, Razzle sat on her little porch watching shooting stars and listening to the surf. It seemed like home—if she ever decided to have one, that is—and she kicked back, feeling entirely in her element. Her mind began wandering over the afternoon at the beach bar—her G&T with lemon, seeing the white rainbow and meeting Wolf. Then, she started thinking about his offer, and slowly her sense of serenity was replaced with uncertainty.

What was she going to do? It would be really fun to work the season at *The Water's Edge,* but what about her degree? Yeah...the dreaded degree. That little piece of paper, the noose around her neck, she'd spent years and a bunch of money on only to find out she had no interest in her stupid, torture-filled course of study. It was probably time to get on board with the general consensus and start acting her age and go get a real job. Even though the idea of it made her want to puke, she supposed she better stop embarrassing her family and herself too, really, and just get on with it.

On the other hand, what if she just carried on as usual, saying screw convention, and took the job at the bar, and then The Boss ignored her all the time? That sure would put a damper on things. And what about Wolf? He was a good looking guy and all, and she got the feeling he dug her too, but what if being in the same space didn't work out? It—*The Water's Edge*—was a precarious situation with the potential of turning terribly awkward, especially as she really needed breathing room without some dude hanging around her all the time. Yeah...probably better not go there...

As Razzle sat there making excuses and predictions of doom and gloom, her anxiety got a little out of hand with all the doubt she was allowing to creep into her brain. But then to her credit, before she got all balled up and had a major meltdown again, she put on the brakes and roped herself in.

"What the hell's wrong with me?" she asked herself out loud. "Why am I ruining my night by being such a tool, sabotaging my own self? I know what I'll do..."

Razzle pulled her legs up, crossing them in her chair, and tuned in...and poof! There she was—the warm, effervescent energy of The Spirit of the Sunflower!

"Hi!" thought-spoke Razzle, overjoyed to have her friend back again.

"Hi! You're doing so well!"

"I am?" asked Razzle dubiously, surprised by the comment, believing herself to be a total train wreck.

"Well, yes. At least you were until just now. But you stopped yourself before you really flipped out, so you're still doing good, silly!"

"Then why do I feel so twisted up?"

"It's because you're compromising yourself. Whenever you go against yourself, you feel unhappy and uncomfortable. But if you're being true to yourself, everything flows, and you feel good. You have to start paying attention to your feelings, so you'll be able to understand what's going on in your head. The reason you feel the way you do right now is because you're lying to yourself, trying to convince yourself of things that aren't right for you and denying who you really are. Remember Shakespeare—*This above all: to thine own self be true.*"

"Ohhhhhhh....I've always wondered what that meant. Is that what everyone's been trying to make me see with all the 'truth' talk?"

"Yes. We're trying to help you understand what you really believe instead of what you *think* you believe. Some of the beliefs you're carrying around are holding you back, and it's time for you to recognize them, so you can release what isn't serving you."

"I won't lie, Razzle. This process can be arduous, and I know you don't care for strenuous mental challenges, but try thinking of it like this. Pretend you're looking at life out of your own personal window. At first the window was wide open because you felt no risks or need for defenses. But as the years passed, you've gradually shut the window and put up bars, feeling the need to protect yourself. These bars are false beliefs. They may have been necessary at one time, but now they've outlived their purpose. And the challenge is that those bars have been there for so long that you don't see them, even though they're right in front of you. You have to remove the bars—your false beliefs—so you can see clearly again."

"But how can I do that if I don't even see the stupid bars or know what my false beliefs are?"

"You don't need to know every single detail exactly. All you need to do is acknowledge their existence, thank them for being a part of your life, understanding they were your creation, but tell them you no longer need them and set them free into the universe. Then you have to make the effort to keep yourself on track."

"Well, it sounds simple enough, but there's still so much I don't get. It's like every time I take a step forward, I take two more back. When am I going to be finished learning this stuff?"

"Never."

"*What???* Are you serious?" How could her friend do this to her, killing here buzz this way?

"We're always becoming, Razzle. Just like the earth turning and the perpetual nature of time, our spirit is infinitely becoming."

"But how am I ever going to—number one—remember everything, and—number two—understand it all?"

"You're clever; you'll figure out a way. But in the meantime, you have to be honest with yourself. It may not be obvious at first what's really bothering you, but if you're truthful, you'll find the source of your discontent, and you can begin to take steps to change the situation."

"Things seemed to be just fine, and I guess I really was making progress...but then I met the cute guy and he offered me that fantastic gig..."

And as Razzle yammered away in self-pity, she heard The Spirit of the Sunflower's infectious laughter poking fun at her good-naturedly. Then she began laughing at herself as well, realizing how dumb she sounded carrying on like a crybaby girl.

"I miss your laugh," she said to her friend.

"The energy of laughter is very powerful. It carries you, lifts you. It's important to keep your sense of humor. You should be enjoying this instead of taking it so seriously, Razzle. You need to lighten up."

"You're so right!"

"Look, don't worry about the *what-ifs;* don't worry about the future. You've got to live in the NOW. If you learned anything from me at all, it should be that."

"Today is the magic, the magic is today", responded Razzle, quoting THE VOICE THAT ISN'T A VOICE.

"That's right," smiled her friend. "Just go with it."

Razzle opened her eyes. The Spirit of the Sunflower was gone, but her words helped bring her back to the moment. Feeling the salty breeze reminded her that this was exactly where she wanted to be, and she went inside to get her notebook.

NOW

# CHAPTER 11

## FEEL YOUR FREEDOM AND FENG SHUI FISH

Dawn broke across Razzle's face, with the first light of day acting like an alarm clock, rousing her from an energizing night's sleep. She jumped out of bed, stuffed her bedhead under her hat and ran straight out to the beach, feet plowing through the cool sand until she reached the water. Then she waded out to her shins and stared at the horizon.

It was one of those overcast mornings where everything in sight was awash in varying monochromatic shades of gray. Dark clouds spread out in all directions, and in the center of the ominous looking sky was a small break where Razzle could see the slit of the sun; its rays radiating out illuminating the whole scene, creating an almost spooky yet entirely transfixing image. She stood in the warm slate colored water and unconsciously lifted her arms, spreading them as wide as she could, embracing all of it.

"FEEL YOUR FREEDOM," she heard THE VOICE THAT ISN'T A VOICE say without the assistance of meditation. And that's exactly what she did, and she really and truly felt it and it was wonderful, like she was completely weightless without a care in the world. She felt—*unblocked.*

Then, without warning, something prickly brushed past her ankles startling her out of her epiphany or whatever it was that was happening. Glancing down, Razzle saw an exotic looking fish with a fabulous silver tail and a chubby orange body weaving in between her legs. It had long black and white whiskers encircling it in the same yin yang pattern as BB's wings, and it was peering up at her through bright green eyes.

As Razzle watched the creature watching her, the fish lifted its head out of the water and proclaimed in the voice of a sage, "I am Feng Shui Fish. And you, my child, have found your balance. This is your Qi...thrown to the wind it scatters, but is retained when encountering water."

Razzle listened respectfully while the venerable fish continued speaking, "Your energy balances best when you are near water. However, this is not the same for everyone. Each individual requires different points of balance, but once discovered and understood, all may achieve inner harmony."

"But I should've seen that ages ago!" Razzle moaned, smacking herself on the head, beside herself for being thick as a brick, failing to realize what should have been apparent long before this if she'd been paying any attention. Instead she'd been subjected to the self-inflicted torment of a dunce!

"Just look at my *List of Little Happinesses!* Almost every single one of them has to do with the beach or the ocean! It was right there in front of me the whole time! Aaaahhhhh!"

"It is true. You have held your answers all along, but you were going outside of yourself for your solutions. When you allow yourself to continuously seek information externally, you inevitably become lost. Now you know better."

Razzle threw her head back, letting out an exasperated groan. She was such a loser! How could she be so blind?

"You must not be too harsh with yourself. Life is complicated, and everyone loses their way at some stage of their journey."

Then Feng Shui Fish pointed his tail toward a small island just offshore that Razzle hadn't noticed before. On it she could see a solitary palm tree flanked on each side by a statue of a fish. "Look at the statues over there," he instructed.

"Those two listened to someone who told them it would be far more glamorous being fish statues on land rather than ordinary old hum-drum fish swimming in the ocean. Now they are miserable. At first they blamed the one who planted the idea for their plight but have since come to understand that they are responsible for their decision. The existence they chose does not agree with them at all, but eventually the ocean will bring them back to where they belong, just like what is happening to you. You also now recognize that another person is never the source of your happiness or unhappiness—it all originates within you. You alone must follow your joy, your inner voice. Do not question it. Let it flow."

"I see what you're saying, but I just can't believe all the time I wasted! Ugh!"

"That is a misguided and thoroughly short-sighted attitude, my girl. How can you say that, especially after all you have experienced along the way to this moment? Read through your notebook. You must remind yourself of all you have learned, and just maybe you will be surprised to discover how this was not really wasted time."

And with that final insightful statement, the phantasmagoric Feng Shui Fish turned, slapped his spectacular silver tail on the top of the water and disappeared into the deep.

Razzle watched the rippling water where the fish had been orating seconds before, thinking about what he'd said and wondering how in the world he knew about her notebook too. But if there was one thing she'd managed to figure out during this wild whirlwind, it was to listen to the advice she was given because so far no one had steered her wrong. So just as the fish suggested, she trudged back to shore to her bungalow where she grabbed her notebook and sat down on the porch to read.

At that very instant the sun, which had completely disappeared during her conversation with Feng Shui Fish, broke free from the clouds, the warmth on her skin reminding Razzle of The Spirit of the Sunflower. Smiling, she said out loud, "Just go with it."

And without really knowing why, instead of starting to read the first page, she flipped to the last blank page of her notebook and began drawing. She sketched the beach and the ocean in front of her, then she put herself in the picture too, standing in the water with her arms reaching out to hug the sky and feel her freedom. When she was done, she looked down at the finished product in shock.

"Did I really do that?" she asked herself dumbfounded. She'd never drawn anything in her life—not since she was a little kid anyway—but she had to admit, it was good. And not only that...she'd loved doing it!

"You allowed your creativity to flow through you," said The Butterfly of Balance, materializing like a phantom, perching on Razzle's shoulder, glowing with pride. "How does it make you feel?"

"Happy," replied Razzle simply, looking into BB's beautiful eyes, returning her smile.

And without another word, the butterfly flew away, leaving the girl in peace to continue with the project she'd yet to realize she'd begun.

# CHAPTER 12

## A Turn of the Wheel and A Spark of an Idea

Razzle was engaged for hours, absorbed with sketching the subjects of interest she'd met over the last few days. She drew BB, The Spirit of the Sunflower, Flamer the Trailblazer, Feng Shui Fish and even the white rainbow. By the time she was done she was googly-eyed and her hand felt like it was about to fall off, but she was tickled in a way she'd never felt before.

Then, all at once, her stomach let out a huge growl, letting her know that breakfast was seriously overdue. So with hunger winning out over creativity for the moment, she took one last admiring look at her artwork and went inside to tidy up.

Razzle walked over to the restaurant and sat down at a table on the patio, and much to her surprise, up strolled the receptionist / chef from the previous evening holding a pot of coffee. "Buenos morning!" she sang out cheerfully. "Java?"

"Yes, please!" laughed Razzle. "You do everything here!"

"Yeah...I get bored doing the same thing all the time, so I've found that if I mix it up, it keeps me entertained."

"Makes perfect sense to me," agreed Razzle.

"I'll be right back with the house breakfast. You get what you get, so don't be upset! Hee-hee!"

What a riot this multi-talented girl is, thought Razzle, loving her style, watching her dance away. While waiting for her mystery breakfast, Razzle savored each sip of her coffee with unbridled enjoyment, inadvertently letting out an audible "Mmmmmmmm......." sharing her passion with anyone within earshot.

For the first time in ages, she was feeling like her old self again, except ten times better. All was right in her world, with everything back to being fun, and she was jazzed with the anticipation of not knowing what was going to happen next.

The bubbly waitress returned in a flash and with graceful efficiency, dropped off a plate of food, refilled Razzle's cup, and after assuring her she'd be back to check on her in a bit, shimmied off to care for other tables. Then with conscious effort, Razzle took her time eating, chewing every bite slowly, concentrating on connecting to each ingredient of her fabulous breakfast.

"I'm practicing being a free flowing eater," she announced to no one, cackling out loud like a madwoman. "I'm such a weirdo," she giggled, amusing herself.

The waitress reappeared just in time to see her table for one sitting there laughing at her empty plate and said, "Guess I don't need to worry about whether or not you're enjoying your breakfast!"

Mortified at being caught acting like a total nutcase, Razzle immediately tried covering it up. "Uh...I was just thinking about this hilarious joke someone told me!" Then before the waitress could ask her what the joke was and trap her in her lie, Razzle hurriedly changed the subject. "Do you happen to know where the closest road is going to *Anywhere*?"

"That would be *The Coast Road*. It's a very picturesque route and in the end will bring you to *Wherever It Is You're Going,* and from there you can figure out your next move. There's also this groovy hillside village along the way you should check out if you have a chance. Some interesting people live there and I bet you'll dig it."

"Thanks a lot. That sounds great. Oh, and by the way, I'll be back to work the season at *The Water's Edge,*" she told her, making the decision right then and there.

"Right on! They have a killer happy hour and the bartender's not too bad either!" said the waitress giving Razzle a knowing wink before introducing herself. "My name is M—short for Michelle. I'm so happy to meet you!"

"Oh..." Razzle gasped, her expression softening at the fond memory of the name. "I had a very special friend with your name once. Funny...you actually remind me of her a little. I'm Razzle Dazzle, but you can call me RD."

"Great name! Well, you're definitely the only Razzle Dazzle I've ever met! And just so you can breathe easy, I'm really good friends with The Boss, so I'll tell him to be nice! His bark is worse than his bite—even though he's a cat! Ha-ha!"

The girls laughed out loud together, causing a few heads to turn in annoyance, but they didn't even notice. "I'd really appreciate that! You must speak Cat then?"

"Doesn't everybody?" asked M, genuinely startled by the question.

"I guess so...at least around here."

Out of the corner of her eye, the acutely aware M saw a man holding his coffee cup over his head and turned in his direction, cutting the conversation short. "Sorry RD, I've gotta run. Have a good trip, but make sure you come see me when you get back. I need a roommate!"

"For sure!" Razzle yelled after her, waving good-bye. Then she stood up and started heading back to her bungalow, smiling to herself and thinking of the new Michelle and the bottomless bag of surprises in this game of life, reflecting in amazement at how—in spite of herself—the wheel just kept on turning.

She returned to her room with every intention of hitting the road, but then suddenly remembered Feng Shui Fish. She was supposed to read through her notebook! She'd gotten so carried away drawing that she'd completely forgotten. So for the second time that morning, she sat down and opened up her notebook, but this time she started from the beginning.

It was almost impossible for Razzle to imagine that she hadn't known BB her whole life instead of only a few days, and she couldn't keep herself from roaring with laughter over her mind boggling introduction to the way-out butterfly back at the crossroad. From there she relived her bumbling first attempt at meditation and hearing THE VOICE THAT ISN'T A VOICE; her bizarre brush with James and his curious limo passengers; reuniting with her lost friend as The Spirit of the Sunflower; her merry-go-round evening with the outlandish Flamer the Trailblazer; and finally, her experience at *The Water's Edge.*

As she read through all her scribbled encounters surrounding her quest to regain her balance, what astounded Razzle, most of all, was how things that used to completely blow her brains out at the beginning were now her new normal. Hmmm, she thought, interesting.

Then she began recapping the morning's events on paper, adding it all to her journal account so she'd be up-to-date. She was in the middle of writing about Feng Shui Fish when she froze, slowly releasing her grip on her pen. She sat motionless, a vacant look replacing the animated expression on her face, as the slow-on-the-draw girl finally began conceiving the inconceivable.

*Holy hell...*She'd been caught up in an honest to God, real life supernatural expedition and now, because of it, her life would never be the same again! Dazed, she flipped to the back of her notebook, staring incredulously at the sketches she'd drawn before breakfast. It was all so unbelievable!

"Seriously, did any of this really happen?" she asked herself, questioning the stability of her sanity once again.

Then Razzle heard BB in her head say, *What appears to be is not what is...*

She inhaled deeply, centering herself and willfully blasting through her mental state of confusion. And as she did, an idea took root in her mind. Maybe—just maybe—she could turn this into a book...

"Housekeeping!"

Oh wow! It was time to check out of there! Pursuing that last thought would have to wait until later. Razzle exhaled a huge sigh of relief, feeling like she'd just dodged a bullet, thankful for the well-timed distraction rescuing her from processing this way too heavy scenario any further, and flashed the just a minute sign to the housekeeping crew.

She ran inside and quickly gathered together her sparse belongings. After securing the knot on her HCC she was good to go, and walked out the door and down the steps to the beach. But before beating feet toward *The Coast Road*, Razzle Dazzle had one more item of business she needed to take care of and began retracing her steps from yesterday—right back to *The Water's Edge Beach Bar* and the hot bartender with the dreamy eyes.

# CHAPTER 13

## COURAGE

As soon as Razzle got to the little beach shack it was plain to see she was a day late and a dollar short. Apparently M hadn't been exaggerating about the big shut-down. *The Water's Edge* was all closed up—no cute bartender, no cranky cat. Looks like I won't be able to do this in person after all, thought Razzle, disappointed not to be getting another look at Wolf.

She tore a piece of paper from her notebook and penned an acceptance letter, letting them know she'd be back to work the season, then folded it in half and slid it under the roll-down door securing the bar. As she was standing back up, she heard a familiar drawl from a disembodied voice say, "I just *KNEW* you had it in you, doll!"

Razzle grinned sheepishly, her face turning as red as her boots, knowing the fire belonging to that voice was keeping an eye on her from somewhere other than the beach bar. She took a long look out over the ocean saluting Flamer the Trailblazer— wherever he was—and pointed herself in the direction of *The Coast Road.*

---

Once again, the receptionist/chef/waitress/new roommate —a.k.a. Super M—proved herself to be a reliable source of information. The route *was* picturesque. As a matter of fact, the scenery was nothing short of breathtaking with the road weaving around the shoreline, rising little by little so that eventually Razzle found herself way up high, walking along the cliff with a view of the magnificent ocean far below. Birds chirped, insects whirred through the air and critters scurried about, dashing across her path and dive-bombing through the branches of the pines and oaks. The wind was blowing lightly, and the overcast sky of the early morning had cleared to a beautiful, cloudless azure blue.

After walking for several hours, Razzle could faintly make out the outline of a tiny village nestled into the side of the cliff up ahead along the snaking road in the distance. It was difficult to judge just how far off it was, but the filtered sunlight was shining down on it like a spotlight and she was pretty sure it was the place M had mentioned, something inside of her saying this was her next destination.

She took her time hiking toward the village, turning over the past few days in her mind, evaluating her new enlightened position. Razzle was forced to admit that her perceptions had been drastically altered and she couldn't hide behind the excuse of ignorance she used to own for being mentally slothful anymore. She'd learned things concerning the world and herself that she'd previously had no clue about, and although the old Razzle would've chosen to ignore its significance, deep down she knew this was no longer an option.

Then she turned to pondering her new-found artistic talent and the blossoming book idea. Why not give it a try? she asked herself. I've got all this sensational material of an adventure ranging from the ridiculous to the sublime complete with an array of wacky characters, and thanks to my creative break-through this morning, I've even got illustrations! Hell, who knows? Maybe this story can even help other unbalanced messes like myself somehow.

It was beginning to make perfect sense. Of course this experience would make a great book, she told herself. All I need to do is put it all together so everyone can follow along. Who-ever came up with the phrase, *truth is stranger than fiction,* hit the nail right on the head with this saga!

She was happily formulating scenarios when, out of no-where, a thought tore through Razzle's consciousness causing her to stop dead in her tracks. *Could this be the book Sonia— the psychic from her very first reading—had told her about???* Ever since that fateful day she'd been carrying around the memory of Sonia's blown-out expression and a notebook and pen, waiting and waiting for an inspiration that never came— until now.

"Oh my God...could this be it?" whispered Razzle, covering her mouth with her hand while her heart and mind raced at the possibility of finally writing whatever it was that Sonia had seen. But her fantasizing came to an abrupt halt as the implications of what she was contemplating hit her full force.

*What am I thinking???????* I can't tell anyone one about this! They'll lock me up and throw away the key! I'll bring shame on my family, all my friends will dump me and the whole world will think I'm out of my mind! And what about my would-be boyfriend, Wolf? He won't want anything to do with a crackpot like me! He'll kick me to the curb in a second, and I can kiss him and my sweet seasonal gig goodbye! This is a nightmare!

And if all that wasn't enough, an even more horrifying likelihood occurred to her. Maybe I actually *have* lost my mind, she thought, a sickening knot tightening in her stomach.

*"Believe in what you believe. It is the truth."*

And although she couldn't see her little guardian angel any-where, knowing BB was cruising around in the ether looking out for her was all the reassurance she needed. She rallied, telling herself to get a grip, and began walking again, thinking maybe a little heart-to-heart with THE VOICE THAT ISN'T A VOICE could help sort her out.

But just as she was pulling herself back together, Razzle rounded a bend in the road and came to another instantaneous standstill. She couldn't believe her eyes...*The Coast Road* was gone! A great big chunk had fallen away, separating one side of the road from the other, and now there was a massive, treacherous drop-off between where she was and the opposite side where she needed to be. She stood staring at the reality of the situation in front of her in wide-eyed bewilderment.

Now what? How could everything that was going so right on this perfect day just go so drastically wrong? She'd come way too far to turn back, and besides, the beach town was sure to be deserted by the time she got there, and she'd have no place to stay anyway. On the other hand, she really wasn't enamored with the alternative idea of plummeting to her death either, and the probability of that made the latter option even less appealing than the former.

"Well if this isn't a sign," she said out loud throwing up her hands, "then I don't know what is." And doing her best to look on the bright side, decided she may as well take this little opportunity to meditate.

So she opened up her HCC and pulled out her well-used sarong, setting herself up right at the edge of the drop-off for effect, then went through her ceremony of preparation and waited...

"Hello," she greeted the presence in her head silently. "Thank you for coming."

"You are welcome."

And before Razzle had a chance to say another word she heard,

"SHINE YOUR GREATNESS ON THE WORLD. GIVE YOURSELF PERMISSION TO BE GREAT. YOU ARE TAUGHT THAT YOU SHOULD BE HUMBLE. YOU ARE TOLD, 'DO NOT BE TOO PROUD OF YOURSELF'. BUT THAT IS WRONG. YOU MUST EMBRACE YOUR GREATNESS. DO NOT BE EM-

BARRASSED BY IT. THERE IS NO REASON TO BRAG OR
BOAST—JUST SHINE."

Razzle opened her eyes, empowered by the clarity of the
information she'd just received. She understood she'd reached
the end of the road—literally—and knew precisely what she
was going to do. The time had come to reconcile this ordeal
and acknowledge its lessons. She'd rebalanced her scales and
now she needed to view herself honestly and objectively,
without judgment, without labels—just as she was—to call a
spade a spade and come clean.

Okay then, she began...

Well to start with, my real name isn't Razzle Dazzle, but I like
it and I'm sticking with it—for the moment. Self-awareness may
not be my strong suit, but this evolution of character is a work-
in-progress, and I'm not ready to go cold turkey just yet, so
Razzle Dazzle I shall remain.

Next, the reason I became lost and unbalanced in the first
place was because I was compromising myself for the sake of
other people, and that's a big fat no-no. I'll never really be
content if I continue doing that because at the end of the day,
I'm in this for myself. In spite of all my relationships—family,
friends, guys, society...whoever—I can never forget my own
importance. My happiness is paramount. I see that now.

Finally then, just for the record, I know I can seem oblivious
at times, but it's just because I want to enjoy life, and I believed
thinking about uncomfortable subjects would only bring me

down. I mean seriously, self-analysis is exhausting, right? And yes, I'm realizing it's necessary and beneficial, but that doesn't make it any less heavy-duty. But I'm trying to change my attitude, and I'm hoping to be less afraid of that stuff from now on. I'm learning there are things I thought I believed that I don't—not truly—and I'm making an effort to correct those false beliefs and replace them with new ones, the real ones.

Oh! There's one last very important thing! I also need to remember to trust myself because nobody knows me better than I know myself—even if I don't have it all figured out yet.

Then Razzle sat for a while, reflecting back over her life and the host of people who'd come and gone. And although there were some occasions where she felt aggravated by her naivety, wishing she could alter a few outcomes, in the end, she was able to see it as the cost of doing business and that understanding gave her a sense of peace and freedom.

"And there you have it," she said out loud, standing up, putting away her sarong and fastening her HCC.

She looked down over the edge of the drop-off. It was a long way to the bottom. Then she gazed across to the other side that seemed so far away and tilted her head back as far as she could, looking up at the sky. And in that moment Razzle realized, "We need each other."

"YES."

"You may have all this great information, but if I don't listen, pay attention and make an effort to use it in my life then it's all wasted. If I choose to ignore all that's happened to me and go back to my old ways, then this entire experience would've been for nothing."

"THAT IS CORRECT."

"Now it's up to me to share—whether anyone listens or not—I have to do it."

And that sudden understanding gave Razzle purpose—a purpose she'd never felt before but knew deep down inside had existed all along. It was the direction she'd been preparing for her whole life. It was where her need to wander came from. It wasn't adventure or experiencing the unknown or meeting new people that propelled her—although all that was awesome. She'd kept on truckin' to find out who she was and man, oh man, had it been an ass-kicking journey! But slowly but surely she was reaching her destination...finally.

"IT WILL TAKE COURAGE TO SHARE THIS WITH THE WORLD."

"I know. But I'll do it."

"Everyone's always telling me how brave I am for going off and traveling by myself, living the way I do. But it's easy to be fearless when you're not scared. If you're not afraid, it's got nothing at all to do with courage. Now *this* is me being brave because it terrifies the hell out of me—oops! Sorry! I mean it terrifies the *daylights* out of me to tell people about all of this. I'm petrified no one will believe me."

And in response, a chorus of voices from the air, the earth, the fire and the water chimed out together in unison, *"They will believe you!"*

Razzle Dazzle smiled. "I understand there's no magic, but this has been absolutely magical. Thank you." And she turned around and walked away from the edge so she could get a running start.

"Here goes everything..."

Then with one hand gripping her hat and the other her HCC, Razzle took off as if she was crazy James the chauffeur himself peeling out in his limo. Running with more power than was humanly possible, her scrawny little chicken legs propelling her to the edge of the cliff where she launched herself forward with all her might, closed her eyes and jumped. And as her red go-go boots left the ground, the last thing she heard was,


"WE WILL NOT LET YOU FALL."

Cowards die many times before their deaths.

The valiant never taste death but once.

Of all the wonders that I yet have heard,

it seems to me most strange that men should fear,

seeing that death, a necessary end,

will come when it will come.


WILLIAM SHAKESPEARE
*JULIUS CAESAR*

## ABOUT THE AUTHOR

Ann Marie Skordy has spent most of her "adult" life traveling and working a series of random and unusual jobs. After graduating college, she bounced around the Caribbean, Hawaii, Japan, Guam, B.C., and Indonesia, and spent years in the cruise ship and private yacht industries. She currently resides in Florida where she eats, drinks gin and tonics with lemon, and makes merry in her own little microcosm at the water's edge. She's also a channel, enjoying both private and collaborative work. She began dabbling as a writer with a children's book, *Start With Your Heart.* This is her first novel. Reach out to her at amskordy@gmail.com.

If you have passion in your heart and a voice for your spirit, then you should have the freedom to share it with others. When you uplift and inspire another through *your* stories of *your* greatness and *your* resilience then you are in your own right a phenom.

Phenom Publishing was created by Dana Sardano and Angela DiMarco for those of you who have something special to offer, something created from your soul and delivered through your heart, something that is yearning to be heard.

Phenom recognizes that within we are *all* phenoms, and through our creativity, we *all* have the ability to change our inner worlds which ultimately changes the world around us. Dana and Angela have begun by sharing their individual stories, and they encourage you to share yours so that humanity can unite and thrive in its phenomenal collective story.

If you have something to share and the voice to share it and are seeking a platform to share it on, join the movement and become the voice of the people.

**Become a phenom.**

Editors@Phenom-Publishing.com

THERE ARE NO COINCIBENCES...

Made in the USA
Middletown, DE
26 February 2023